MW00967075

FETCHING
JONAS BLAKE

MARGARET McKINNEY

FETCHING
JONAS BLAKE

TATE PUBLISHING
AND ENTERPRISES, LLC

Fetching Jonas Blake
Copyright © 2011 by Margaret McKinney. All rights reserved.

No part of this publication may be reproduced, stored in a retrieval system or transmitted in any way by any means, electronic, mechanical, photocopy, recording or otherwise without the prior permission of the author except as provided by USA copyright law.

This novel is a work of fiction. Names, descriptions, entities, and incidents included in the story are products of the author's imagination. Any resemblance to actual persons, events, and entities is entirely coincidental.

The opinions expressed by the author are not necessarily those of Tate Publishing, LLC.

Published by Tate Publishing & Enterprises, LLC
127 E. Trade Center Terrace | Mustang, Oklahoma 73064 USA
1.888.361.9473 | www.tatepublishing.com

Tate Publishing is committed to excellence in the publishing industry. The company reflects the philosophy established by the founders, based on Psalm 68:11,
"The Lord gave the word and great was the company of those who published it."

Book design copyright © 2011 by Tate Publishing, LLC. All rights reserved.
Cover design by Shawn Collins
Interior design by Sarah Kirchen

Published in the United States of America

ISBN: 978-1-61346-488-5
1. Fiction / General
2. Fiction / Historical
11.10.03

This story is dedicated to all the girls left behind
while the boys go to seek their glory.

ACKNOWLEDGMENTS

I would like to thank, in this order: my daring and generous God (the giver of dreams); my husband, Alan (who never nagged); my best friend, Jillian (who nagged just enough); my mother, Marylee (the ultra-grammarian); and the good people at Tate Publishing.

PREFACE

VIRGINIA, SEPTEMBER 1775

The last time I saw Jonas Blake, he was walking away from me, proudly showing me his back after I'd entreated him countless times to stay.

It was September, the last warm days finally slipping away, making room for the first frosty days of fall. I'd followed him down the lane to beg him to remain on our farm, or at the very least, not to go to the militia.

Which was worse? The thought of forever enduring his anger and hurt, or knowing that he was off in a mad rush to fight the British? I would far prefer he live a commonplace life, safe, albeit not with me, than see him killed by a cursed redcoat. But Jonas would forge ahead to make his way in the world, armed with the courage supplied by his generous God.

I clutched his arm, wordless, because I knew there was no use pleading anymore. I began to cry, and Jonas looked away. When he spoke, his voice was icy enough to give me shivers.

"Good-bye, Anne."

"Are you really going then? To Sussex?"

He laughed, the sound grating rather than mirthful.

"No, Anne. Not Sussex. The county militia would not afford me the opportunities I'm seeking. No, I believe I'll go to Williamsburg, to join the *real* action."

"Williamsburg?" Even I, under-acquainted with the mechanics of the war, understood his meaning. The realization of his plans made me fearful.

"Haven't you heard, Anne? Williamsburg is a *fool's* paradise," he said, wrenching his arm away. He turned from me, pulling up the corners of his tan field coat against the breeze that signaled the coming evening. Jonas began to walk down the lane, away from our farm. I stood stock-still in my place. He turned east, away from our small village toward Williamsburg and toward war.

PART ONE:
THE PREDICAMENT

IN WHICH THE POTATOES
ARE LEFT UNATTENDED

RURAL VIRGINIA, MAY 1777

The solitude of the endless, dusty planting season had schooled me in studiously avoiding my sister.

"Anne! Anne!"

Betsy's voice floated across the May breeze to the south fields, where I was on my knees in the earth. A basket of pared potatoes sat to my right, my only companion on this long, tiring morning. The dawn awoke me; I was out feeding the animals before breakfast, before any tea or victuals for myself. The silence of our farmhouse afforded plenty of opportunity for feelings of resentment and self-pity to make their appearance, but I had neither the time nor the energy to waste on them, so they were put to rest. The sight of the sun rising over the fields of Summerton Farm certainly helped—I couldn't help but feel proud of my family's land on such a brisk May morning, and with renewed vigor I determined to see it safe and well cared for. And right now, the only person available to provide good care was me.

"Anne! Anne, where *are* you?"

Pausing in my digging, I perked an ear to listen…no, I wouldn't answer. Betsy often shouted at me across the fields with very little reason. She could wait. Burrowing my hands deep into the moist soil, I resumed my task. Potatoes were the easiest crop to grow—they didn't require seeds or money to order seeds or trips into town to buy seeds. They required only old potatoes, cached throughout the fall and winter months, pared around each fertile eye, and planted after the last frost, which in Sussex County was the middle of May. I myself was not fond of potatoes, but I could spend hours pondering a litany of foods that I preferred. In my months of working and planting and sowing, my busy and hungry brain was prone to concocting elaborate meals filled with foods not seen around here in an age: rich puddings, boiled seafood, Welsh rarebit... I was even fantasizing about food from England, a country I had never seen nor visited.

My thoughts had turned to strawberry sauce when my twin brother, Tom, interrupted me. "Anne."

I jumped and glanced up at him, squinting in the midday sun. At seventeen, Tom stood a full six feet. His hair, kept short by a merciless Betsy and her kitchen shears, was a tawny yellow, like wheat. The rough breeches he wore needed mending, and the sleeves of his homespun shirt were too short, ending halfway up his useless right arm. An accident at the well when he was seven years old rendered his right arm and leg virtually powerless; the doctor said that the muscles on that side of his body simply stopped working. My father, deeply eager for a strapping son to run his farm, was devastated. My mother worried that he would never find a wife. For my part, I loved Tom like a twin sister should, for he was the other half of my own self. Tom did what he could to help around our farm, but his abilities were quite limited. However, a wonderful sense of humor and an indomitable spirit gave me all the help I needed.

"Have you been out here all morning?" Tom's eyes, gray like my own, were dancing merrily. It gave him no end of pleasure to play the devil's advocate between my sister and me. "Is Mistress Betsy driving the whip again?"

I wiped the clean part of my apron across my eyes, which were now watery from staring into the sun too long. "The potatoes won't plant themselves, Tom," I retorted. With Tom alone could I let my guard down and allow my burden to show. Betsy's constitution wasn't built for conflict and difficulty, but Tom was made of stronger stuff; he could handle it. True to form, he cast me a good-natured grin.

"Of course not, Annie. That's why we're so lucky to have you."

A smile played on my lips despite distaste for my nickname.

"Well, go on, Tom. State your business." I resumed my digging, glancing with dismay at the acres of fields left to plant. How could we keep crops in them?

"Betsy needs you."

"So I've heard."

"It's serious, Anne. Norrington came to call again."

Icy-cold shivers worked down my spine. My breath quickened as I scanned Tom's face for information. His mouth was still, serious, but revealed nothing. I sighed and hauled myself from my dirt hole, brushing my skirts off. Tom turned wordlessly and limped back toward our house, his right foot dragging as he walked. I fell into step beside him, letting the silence hang for a few uneasy minutes before I would have to deal with the horror that was Will Norrington.

"Is he still there?" I held my breath.

Tom shook his head.

Sussex County, Virginia, along with the neighboring counties, was a skeletal mix of women, children, and old men. Most men of useful age were gone to war. For two years now, the battle against the British continued in pockets and skirmishes, mostly to our north. From what we'd heard, things went badly for the rebels, but we collectively prayed that our men would somehow bring the British tyranny to an end.

We of the Commonwealth of Virginia had been slow to warm to the idea of *revolution*. Despite having produced some of the era's greatest patriots, in the tidewater region we were farmers first, nationals second. As long as there were crops to plant and harvest and a ready market, we could be content. Sussex County was not littered with tobacco farms, but rather with vegetables and grain—crops that were needed and desired in the Indies and other parts of the colonies.

As the cause drew on, however, and the British clung to its mercantilist ideals, we farmers had to alter our opinions. For the British were dead-set on working the colonies down to the nub to benefit *them*—the Mother Country. And we, a fledging colony of gentleman agrarians, were hard-pressed to understand why that had to be so. Why could we not maintain a pleasant relationship with the British without their taking advantage of our hard work and lush soil? And so Williamsburg and its environs, like Boston before it, exploded in patriotic fervor, causing nerves abundant in its governor, Lord Dunmore, and a steady stream of volunteer soldiers when needed.

As a result, all of our young, able farmhands trickled away one by one, lured by the adventure of war. With Father being ill and Tom crippled, the bulk of the work fell to Betsy and me. We still engaged one longtime hand, Sam, but he was older than Father and was much less handy than even I.

Tom and I arrived at the farmhouse breathless and grim. Our small house was relatively new; our parents had come from England twenty years earlier, acquired some land, and started farming. The house was small, because Father had preferred to save money for more land. The intent was to add more rooms as the years wore on, but Father's illness had prevented all such tasks.

Mother and Father met and fell in love in Sussex, England, in 1756. My father, Richard, who was the youngest son of minor gentry, had no expectation of title or large inheritance, so at the age of twenty-five he asked his father, hat in hand, for enough money to sail to America and start a farm. His father, William Summerton, a true English gentleman, had no interest in coming to America himself, but admired the spirit and courage of his lastborn and agreed to finance his life in a new land.

My mother, Elizabeth, was the daughter of a clergyman. She was the eldest and most beautiful of his daughters. In an age where ladies were almost as meticulously educated as the gentlemen, my mother could sing, paint, speak three languages, embroider, make her own clothes, and play the harp *and* the pianoforte. It was a bygone conclusion that she captivated my father. And she fell so much in love with *him* that she was willing to leave her popularity and social status to join him abroad. She had no idea what would await her in Virginia, but hard work and little society. Only her love for Father prevented bitterness from seeping into their marriage—instead, she poured all of the stolen glory from her youth into Betsy.

Indeed, the balls and cotillions and coming out parties that were curtailed by her rapid marriage to my father were arranged for Betsy, along with every new dress pattern, the prettiest bonnets, and hours spent before the mirror attempting new feats with Betsy's tawny locks. Imagine my mother's chagrin when she found Abbingdon lacking in society and nary a ball to be found. Still, her efforts were not lost on my sister, who retained the prettiest of feminine wiles and the loveliest of manners, even in these war-torn times.

Betsy stood on the wide porch, wringing her hands. Nearly nineteen, she appeared older by her worn clothing and pinched expression. My sister would have been beautiful if our parents had but stayed in England. She had the same flax-colored hair as Tom and me, but while our eyes were gray, hers were bluish-violet like Mother's. Her frame was tall and pleasantly round, while mine was all bones and angles, and she was altogether more sweet natured than both of her siblings. However, the recent years of lean eating, ceaseless worrying, and constant housework robbed her of her bloom.

"Oh, stop your fretting, Betsy," I snapped, bounding up the steps and pushing past my sister into the kitchen. My default reaction to

Betsy and her incessant fretting was annoyance, but it was important to bridle my tongue and save her the needling. Sometimes, when my mind finished its trolling through the standard thoughts, wishes, and worries that occupied my daily tasks, I felt sorry for Betsy. Looking over an ailing farm and a dying father was no life for her. Back in England, other girls our age were embroidering cushions, painting, learning French, or other useless nonsense. Betsy would both excel in and enjoy such a life.

Although it was midday in May, there was still a kitchen fire—it was necessary for our father, and I didn't mind it myself. I stood at the hearth for a few seconds, letting Tom calm Betsy down before they joined me in the kitchen. When they arrived, Betsy was the picture of serenity, and Tom looked exhausted by his efforts to that end.

"Tea, Anne?" Betsy offered primly. She lifted the kettle and poured me a cup. I sat wearily at the thickly planed table, where I'd shared family meals my entire life. I watched Betsy prepare the tea prettily, as if I were her treasured guest. The Stafford tea service was my mother's most prized possession, given as a wedding gift from her mother, painstakingly packed and coddled on the crossing, and hand-washed twice daily throughout my youth. Betsy preserved my mother's elegant manners, insistent on creating a lovely and graceful teatime, even if the refreshments were scarce.

"Thank you, Betsy," I said. "I am sorry I snipped at you. You know how Norrington wrenches my nerves."

Betsy's eyes widened in fear, but she visibly soothed under Tom's calming hand on her arm.

"Oh, yes, Anne, mine too."

"Well, you might as well tell me about it, Betsy. Do go on."

My sister's voice was weak, wavering in alarm. "He said we had until the first of July to see if Father was going to revive. If he doesn't, he will force us to sell the farm, and we shall have to move."

The panicked breath I had been holding down in my stomach whooshed unbidden out of my mouth. It was plain that Father was not going to get better. The last eight months were spent keeping the severity of his illness a secret for this very reason.

Mother had died suddenly—the doctor said she suffered from a stroke. It was a horrible shock to my father and wholly unbelievable to the three of us. The event happened not long after Jonas left, and the wound was still open. My mother and I shared very few words of civility in the months before her passing. Ill feelings and unforgiveness would forever hang between us.

If it was difficult on me, it was thrice the pain for Father. In the ensuing months, we watched him dwindle day-by-day, taking little food or drink, feeling few enjoyments about the farm, and seldom speaking to us. We each tried in our own way to encourage him and bring him joy, to ease him out of his depression, but he simply wasn't willing. He was a shell of a man for months on end, and one day he simply collapsed in the parlor. We struggled with him up the stairs to his bed, and the days since were spent tending him. He rarely spoke, but Betsy harassed him into taking tea and broth several times a day. Occasionally he ate solid food and even moved around, shifting his position in the bed to see out the window. However, the virile, commanding presence of our youth was gone—gone the day my mother was buried beside the village church.

So there we were, Tom, Betsy, and I, miserably biding our time until he died, and when that happened, Summerton Farm would be lost, our only home stolen from us.

In the years since the war began, men were leaving Abbingdon in a steady stream. Some returned after a year of service, but many never returned. Those that died, or simply stayed away, left property to tend and only widows to do it—widows that were sometimes young and inexperienced, often with small children to add to their burden. Some women were older and hardier, but even they didn't always have a fierce attachment to their land. The circumstances left our village with several once-prosperous farms in disarray, their distraught owners ready and willing to sell their land to whoever would take it.

William Norrington was an answer to prayer for many in such a state. His business began unobtrusively—he bought a farm here or there, unloaded it rather, from a poor widow with no idea how to handle her acreage. But Mr. Norrington had broader plans than that of answering prayers. He relished the thought of owning the extent of our farms, using his friends to work the land and supply the army for a handy profit. It was almost feudal—one man in charge of thousands of acres of land, all farmed by cheap labor and completely for his own monetary benefit. If he achieved ownership of Abbingdon, what would stop him from buying the farms along the road to Carlton twenty miles away?

The war dragged on, Abbingdon's husbands, fathers, and sons stayed away, and Norrington continued to purchase local land. He owned all of the land surrounding Summerton Farm and was interested in adding our acreage to his kingdom. Ever the gentleman, he never made an offer or showed any interest while Mother was alive—Father was well then. And when Mother died last year, Norrington bade his time, coming over once to offer his condolences. He even sent some stores and kind wishes, but never did he mention buying our farm.

It was only in the past eight months, when Father ceased his weekly trip into town for supplies, that Norrington began asking questions. "What's ailing old Richard Summerton? We haven't seen him at the feed store in an age. Wonder if things are well over at Summerton Farm? You know, I hear he never quite recovered from his wife's death ... it's a shame too, him with those daughters, and no mama to raise them."

When word leaked into town that Father was actually ill, nay, taken abed, Norrington's visits became more regular, his manner more intense in its inquiry.

Now, finally, Will Norrington had staked his claim, giving us an ultimatum.

"Barely a month." I sighed into my tea. *Please, God, no,* I prayed halfheartedly. *I beg you to help my family out of this.* I talked to God seldom and always in worry tinged with bitterness.

"What can we do, Anne?" Tom asked, his usually jovial face now grave.

"Well, we don't have enough hands to make the place profitable," I said. "Too much of our land is going to be fallow this year as it is. We'll barely grow enough food to put away for the winter."

"But we own our land, don't we?" Tom asked. "I mean, isn't it ours?"

"Of course it is! Father isn't one to borrow anything."

Our father, when he was well, always had plenty to say on the subjects of honor, integrity, and frugality. Indeed, before the war, when our land was robust and we had a dozen young men working it for us, Father was always preaching to them about saving their wages. I couldn't imagine that he would have bought anything he couldn't pay for with actual coin.

"It doesn't really matter, anyway," Tom said to himself, as though answering his own question. "Last week Mary Hudgins told me that when Norrington bought her cousin's place, he showed up with a passel of armed men. He presented a paper to sign and a bag of money. Poor Mary said her aunt had to sign the deed with Will's rifle casually pointing at her."

"Well, that's just horribly unfair!" I cried, pushing back my chair and pacing around the kitchen. "Who does he think he is? We're still an English colony—not some lawless wasteland." I turned toward the fire, placing my hands square on the mantel, forcing the panic back down into my throat.

"It's war, Annie," Tom answered. "There are no men here to stand up to him. Nobody would dare cross him and that posse of his. The magistrate is too busy dealing with supplies and worrying about the British."

Norrington was always with a band of large and capable men—rumor was that they started in the militia up north, but were thrown out for uncomely character. Their leader, the nasty Ben Cummings, followed Norrington around as one would a general, and his knife could always be seen glinting from its place at his belt.

"And you know he has more money than anyone," Tom continued. "He *owns* this town." His last words were uttered with such dejection, I wheeled around and pointed a finger at him.

"Don't you lose hope on me, Thomas Summerton. I can't have you giving up. We will find a way out of this."

Tom awkwardly lifted himself from his chair and shuffled across the room to me. He put his arm around my shoulders.

"Annie, we either need a whole heap of money or a posse of our own. Otherwise, come July first, he's coming in here and taking our farm."

Tom's words resonated louder than all of Betsy's wailings, because they were coming from my steadfast friend and ally.

"Money…" I said to myself, "or a posse of our own."

"Anne?" Betsy whispered, silent thus far through our heated discussion.

I turned from my musings. "Yes?"

"Do you think you could rush your wedding to Nate?"

IN WHICH I TAKE A SPILL

SUMMERTON FARM, MARCH 1775

"Anne, can you take this food out to the farmhands?"

My mother's voice pulled me from my book. I wasn't supposed to be reading novels, but Mary Hudgins snuck one to me last week in church, and it was so riveting I couldn't put it down. It was a long, dramatic affair, complete with a devastatingly handsome count, a winsome heroine, and a dastardly villain. How could I do anything useful when such a novel existed? I sat in the front parlor, my back to my mother—she was busy in the kitchen and thought I was sewing.

"Anne"—her voice came sharply now—"you'd better not be reading."

Quickly, I shoved the small, leather-bound wonder under my sewing.

"Yes, ma'am." I leaped from the couch, pulling on my gaiters and a thick hooded cloak. Although it was technically spring, there was still a bothersome layer of slush on the ground, causing a distressing amount of mud. Taking lunch to the farmhands was one of my daily tasks and lately held a certain and particular pleasure for me. I hummed to myself as I latched the toggles on my cloak, swirling into the kitchen where my mother waited with a thick tray of biscuits and sliced ham.

"Now, Anne, don't dawdle." She handed me the tray. "You know how difficult it is for Father to keep the farmhands focused while you're dancing about. It's difficult enough to train them as it is."

"Yes, ma'am," I repeated automatically, my legs dropping into a curtsey.

"Elizabeth," Father called from the mudroom, "perhaps you should stop sending the girls to take lunches to the men. Send Tom instead."

"Oh, stuff and nonsense," my mother said. She glanced out the window at Tom, who was following Sam to the barn. A quick look of sadness crossed her face as she watched him carry a hoe, dragging his right foot behind him. "He can hardly wield the tray. Besides, Betsy draws the attention around here. Nobody's going to pay heed to Anne."

I stifled a giggle. Such things were of little concern to me. I was fifteen that spring, Betsy sixteen, and while she certainly had her fair share of admirers, I had no interest in stuffy boys from town. They weren't nearly interesting enough.

Father entered the kitchen, planting a kiss apiece on Mother's and my cheeks. He looked me over approvingly; although Betsy, with her rosy beauty, was the apple of my mother's eye, my father was partial to my plucky spirit and buoyant attitude. My mother—not as much. We usually butted heads on … well … everything. I was much too free-spirited and uninterested in our home to please her. Betsy was, indeed, the perfect lady in our family. She was the picture of our mother, with her creamy skin and violet eyes and dimpled elbows. Already a favorite among the town boys, Mother was training her to be the ideal wife, hoping she would be fought over like a prize cow. The thought of it made me giggle. I was still too young to be ferreted out as a wife and had no interest in it anyway. If I had my way, my days would be spent outside amongst our fields, reading forbidden books and eating the apples from Mr. Carter's grove across our north pasture. "Altogether too wild," I once overheard Mother say about me, and I would have it no other way.

"Be careful on the slush, Anne," my mother warned—again. "We don't need you dropping those biscuits all over the yard."

"Fine, fine," I said under my breath. My mind was already back in my book, which was safely hidden in my sewing basket.

My father employed a number of hired hands during the spring and summer months, and into the fall harvest when our farm was at its busiest. Most of them were transients, many from the north, stopping in Virginia for the warm weather. We occasionally had boys from neighboring villages, shipped away from their own homes as punishment for some sort of secret trouble. Although the thought of secret trouble piqued my curiosity something terrible, I generally paid the boys no heed. Most of their attention was focused on Betsy, and for the most part, they were dull and stupid.

But one was different.

I picked my way carefully over the slushy ground toward the barn, where my father would have the hands sharpening the blades of the plow or pitching hay into the loft for our grumpy old horse. April, the beginning of the planting season for us, was rapidly approaching—the ground was still frozen, but there was plenty of preparation work to do. And nobody was better prepared for *anything* than my father.

The barn door stood open, which wasn't well thought, given how cold it was outside. I shuffled about before entering—it wasn't proper to enter the barn, where most of the hands slept, unannounced. A lady at my core, I paused there and hallooed.

"Excuse me, gentlemen?"

No answer for several seconds. With my *proper* ministrations unheeded, I ceased trying to be dainty and engaged a practical volume instead.

"Dinner!"

"Come in, Miss Anne," came a chorus of voices from inside. I rolled my eyes and edged my elbow against the door, inwardly grumbling that none of them could be bothered to help me with the tray. My arm pushed against the heavy wood, which stuck fast in the mud and slush. *No wonder they left it open*, I thought, trying to wedge my body into the small opening. Suddenly and very unfortunately, I felt my foot slipping on the ice, along with my grip on the tray of food.

"Oh, *blast* it!" I squealed as I pitched forward. My mother's warning echoed in my head as I watched the tray slide down, powerless to stop it.

"Whoa, easy there, Anne!" a male voice said. One callused hand gripped the end of the biscuit tray; the other caught my cloaked elbow before my body hit the ground. I regained my balance, pulling my foot into the barn and setting it securely on the dry dirt floor. When my wits returned, I noticed I had one end of the tray, and Jonas Blake held the other.

A hot blush leaped across my face. "Oh, Mr. Blake...I thank you."

"Why, you are welcome, Miss Anne," always the sardonic tone simmering in his words.

Jonas Blake was easily the most accomplished and intelligent of my father's farm hands this year—I'd heard Father praise him many times during our family meals. His mother and sister had a house in Abbingdon, but Jonas boarded with us like the other hands and was immensely helpful to our farm. He was tall and well built—which Father needed. And he was quick-witted and interesting—which I adored. Jonas and I had shared many a laugh at the expense of my family (usually my sister) or the other farmhands. He knew I was always available for a joke and a secret smile. I looked forward to these conversations immensely. True, he was eighteen and probably didn't even consider me beyond that of a little sister, but that was to be understood. Jonas was my friend, and I was delighted he was there.

One thing I enjoyed about Jonas was his willingness to listen to my prattle. The week before, my father sent him inside the house to reinforce a splintered beam in our parlor. My mother was resting upstairs in her bedroom, and Betsy wouldn't dare to be seen below stairs with a farmhand. However, I found myself seated on a low stool at his feet the whole of the afternoon, handing him nails and sharing with him all the workings of my mind.

First, I told him that my mother had chastised me for reading novels.

"Well, Anne, I don't disagree with Mrs. Summerton there. You could use a smattering of God's Word, you know."

Second, I told him that I'd overheard Edward Hudgins saying Betsy was the prettiest girl in Abbingdon.

"She *is* quite pretty, Anne, but you are equally so."

And then I asked him why he worked for us, when he was plainly so clever he could most likely do anything he pleased.

He had no ready answer for that; he just glanced at me sideways and grinned. "Clever, is it? Well, I couldn't say much about that, Anne, but I do know that a man cannot really be a man unless he feels useful—until he shows his mettle, proves his worth. Do you understand my meaning?"

I didn't, not then.

"You are just barely a man, Jonas," I said. "Not yet nineteen."

To this he laughed heartily and tugged my braid, which had come loose from its coil. "I am the provider for my family, Anne, and that makes me a man no matter what my age may be."

"Provider? What happened to your father, Jonas?"

A dark cloud passed over his blue eyes at my bold inquiry. His brow furrowed, and he was silent so long I thought he wouldn't answer. Indeed, I nearly apologized for asking when he spoke abruptly.

"He left us when I was a boy. Told my mother he had no use for us. We were *weighing him down.*" His tone told me he'd speak no more on the subject. I stood and stepped next to him, placing my hand on his arm and giving it a gentle squeeze.

"You're right useful to us, Jonas," I whispered.

He patted my hand and smiled. "Well, that's worth something, ain't it?"

I grinned and regained my seat at his feet while he resumed his task. "Jonas?"

"Yes? More questions, little one?"

Although I desperately wished to be considered his equal, it did please me so when he called me "little one."

"D'you think we will go to war with the British?"

No hesitation this time.

"Yes, I do, Anne."

Now, I had heard talk of the war umpteen times between my mother and father, always in low, hushed tones, and often when walking through the village, but I had never had an actual adult conversation about it with anyone.

"Do you think we *should* go to war?"

At this, Jonas bit his lip, stalling. He glanced at me sidelong, his light brown hair brushing over his forehead. "Why do you wish to know, Miss Curious? You planning on fighting with the militia?"

"No." I shifted uncomfortably. "I just need to know if our family is Tory or Patriot."

He chuckled. "Your father holds his cards close to his chest, Anne, but I'd wager he's a Patriot."

"Why?"

Jonas took on a whole new air of excitement and purpose as he spoke these next words—he seemed uncomfortably revolutionary to me. "Because, Anne, your father is far too interested in a man's personal liberty to allow another to trample it. And that's what the British government has been aiming to do for some time now—trample our own liberty by controlling us."

My eyes narrowed in suspicion. "How do you know what the British are trying to do, Jonas?"

"I read the papers, Anne. Here in Virginia we've got us some of the best Patriots in the colonies, and they write essays and papers and send 'em out for all of us Americans to read. To give us hope."

"Hope," I murmured.

Now, I was fifteen years old and had no serious thought beyond my next chance to be idle, but that first brush of mature, equal conversation with Jonas stayed with me. I pondered it while I was alone, during the times when I usually scurried to a hiding place with a novel. A mere child of fifteen with no cares in the world, I found myself contemplating the blessed beauty of being free—be that free from tyranny, free from burdens, or free from our own nonsensical ways.

If I may say so, my first strains of maturity pushed through that day, like early shoots in the spring vegetable garden, and I owed it to Jonas.

"Miss Anne," Jonas said, interrupting my thoughts in the drafty barn, "why don't you let me take that tray for you?"

I awoke from my short reverie. He was staring at me intently, his blue eyes amused. And then Jonas began to laugh. I found myself the center of attention for the whole of the barn and its inhabitants. It embarrassed me, and my weakness made me angry. After all, his humor was supposed to be shared with me, not directed at me. His disregard made me feel childish and small—the most unsavory feelings for a tender, young girl. I had to salvage my dignity as best I could, which entailed employing my pride.

This in mind, I dropped the tray in his hands, lifting my chin haughtily and fixing Jonas with a withering glare.

"Thank you, *Jonas*," I said coolly, knowing my use of his first name was ill bred. The other boys left their tasks and made their way over to the food hungrily. The biscuits were discovered, and I was no longer needed.

"Many thanks, Miss Anne," six young men mumbled around their food. I nodded politely, backing slowly to the barn door. Jonas was standing still; he had yet to take a biscuit from the tray. My eyes met his briefly, and for the first time I saw something flicker in their blue depths.

"Anne!"

My eyes somehow rolled themselves up to the ceiling automatically at the sound of my mother's shrill voice. She always managed to summon me just when I was comfortable. I was seated by the fire in the parlor, ripping out stitches on my blue bonnet, as Betsy promised to show me how to add ribbon to the brim to make it look smarter. Clothing and accessories, or more specifically, how to wear them well and look nice, had not interested me much until this past spring. However, recent additions to the Summerton farm had inspired me, and honestly, I needed all the help I could get.

"Anne!"

With a *humph*, I threw my sewing back into my basket and flounced into the kitchen. When I saw what she was assembling, my good spirits quickly sank.

"Oh, no, Mother, not the tea tray."

Sure enough, my mother had assembled the afternoon tea on a massive tray, complete with sandwiches, biscuits, and a large earthenware crock of the steaming beverage. And just as sure, I was expected to take it across the icy field to the barn. After my comedic entrance with the biscuit tray the day before, I was reluctant to even chance it.

"Really, mother? The tea tray? It's so heavy."

My mother waved her hand dismissively.

"You're a stout girl, Anne. Just mind your step."

I groaned and fetched my cloak, pulling up my hood and donning my gloves. Next I had to locate my gaiters and pull them on over my boots. Could the farmhands not come to the house and fetch the tea tray themselves? Of course, there was the one consolation in the matter, for I was always eager to see Jonas Blake. Although he had treated me poorly the day before, and I him, I was eager to forgive him and see in what mirthful chat we could engage that day.

My winter things applied, my mother held the door open while I hefted the large tray and crept carefully over the field to the barn. This time, rather than try to edge through the door unattended, I kicked the barn door soundly and made my presence known.

"Gentlemen!" I hollered, in a most unladylike fashion. "Teatime!"

A flurry of young men rushed to the door, pulling it open and helping me inside. I glanced around the barn quickly, searching for Jonas. He was seated quietly in the corner, a book in his hand, probably the Bible. One thing I'd learned about Jonas, he was always reading the Bible. I stood about, watching the hands tear into the tea and refreshments, waiting for Jonas to walk over and greet me, like he always did. And then a diverting exchange would follow, resulting in my great amusement and delight. I could return to the parlor and fix my bonnet with a secret smirk.

Only today, Jonas remained in his corner. He did not lay his book aside, nor did he join the rest of the hands at the tea tray. In his chair he continued to sit, reading his Bible. I was utterly dismayed; for the first time in months Jonas had let an opportunity at conversation pass.

I was not the only person who noted Jonas's absence. Edward Hudgins, another farmhand and brother to my good friend Mary, called out, "Jonas, halloo there! You're about to lose your share of the tea, my friend."

Jonas looked up from his Bible with a ready smile. He scanned the faces of his cohorts with easy humor; however, when his eyes met mine, the levity fled his face, and at once he became somber. A slight inclining of the head, a mumbled, "Good day, Miss Anne," and he returned to his reading.

I nodded in return, edging nearer and grinning in hopes to draw him out. "Mr. Blake, come! Would you not care for some tea?"

When he raised his eyes from his book, he addressed the other man, "No, thank you, Edward, you carry on. Enjoy the biscuits." And with that, he returned to his Bible, and I returned to my parlor, dejected and dismayed.

IN WHICH I
EXERCISE MY HORSE

MAY 1777

Nathaniel Wilkins and I were betrothed. We were to marry sometime in the fall.

He asked me a fortnight ago, after we were dismissed from the small church that sat in the center of Abbingdon. Nate lived in nearby Carlton, only seven miles away. The Wilkins family had a large farm in Carlton, and there was no danger of it falling into the hands of Will Norrington. Nate's father, Jack, was fiercely attached to his land, and completely uninterested in helping to fight the British soldiers.

"It's not our war, Annie," he'd whispered to me countless times when the talk of the town turned to the war. "I'm staying put here on my land so that it will still be here for my boy."

Nate was a nice enough young man—nineteen, hard working, and very intelligent. He was well built, though not so tall as my brother, clean, and relatively handsome. Actually, his dark brown eyes were uniquely beautiful, and he was altogether a pleasing person.

We had been carrying on a respectable friendship for an age already. He was quieter than other boys, shy mainly, not stupid, but when we did talk the conversation was always satisfying. When the war began, and the men on our farm began to seep away, Nate slowly made his way into my life, step by cautious, unassuming step. We walked home from church together on Sundays and Wednesdays. He carried my packages from the village sometimes, especially if Tom couldn't come to help me. Occasionally, his father stopped at our farm to bring us a side of ham or some eggs, particularly during this past winter when my father's absence from village life became so glaring.

I was grateful for his attention—by the early spring I knew our family situation was severe, and that I was the sole person able to fix it. But more than that, it was nice to be somebody's beau, rather than somebody's mother or sister or caretaker. Nathaniel made me feel like his girl long before I even realized he was courting me.

The day he proposed was a warm spring day, warm enough for the families of Abbingdon to linger after church in the midday sun. As planting season had not yet begun, my siblings and I spent the past months in our close kitchen near the fire. I was constantly going over the accounts and wondering how much food we could buy on credit, while Betsy persistently fussed over Father. It was altogether a gloomy way to spend the season, so I was happy to sit outside our church and bask in the warmish sunlight. The change in seasons was welcome, hopeful for me.

Betsy and Tom were talking to Mary Hudgins, while others of our acquaintance milled around the churchyard. We'd heard little news of the war; in a way we felt fortunate that our homes had not been ravaged by battle, and that most of our men—away serving in the militia, or some in the Continental Army—were still alive. However, the pace of life was drearier, less joyful, with a war afoot.

"And what secret thoughts are occupying you on such a beautiful day, Miss Anne?" Nate had approached me silently, in that unassuming way of his. He leaned up against the tree where I was sitting, his hands in his pockets, his way peaceful. Nate was always serene—I never saw a bit of striving in his personality, just quiet and steady strength.

"Nothing of consequence, Mr. Wilkins," I responded. "In fact, it would be pleasant to have a partner in conversation, if you please."

He inclined his head with a smile. Turning his gaze to my siblings, he cocked his head in their direction.

"Your brother seems to think a great deal of Miss Hudgins."

Nate's assertion brought a smile to my face. Mary was a good neighbor and a lively friend—pretty, with very pleasing manners. Her manners were especially pleasing when Tom was near.

"That is true, Mr. Wilkins," I said. "Mary is quite popular on our farm, and Tom is the best of young men."

Nate waited quietly before introducing a new topic, and the topic he chose was a major shock to my worn self.

"Miss Anne, I know you're having a difficult time at the farm without your father up and about." He paused to kneel down next to me, his proximity providing new and unexpected nervousness. "I can't tell you how it wears on me to think of you on that big farm alone, the work and worry all fallen to you since your … father's unfortunate illness."

I simply nodded, summoning the strength to hold my tears back and appear dignified. Nate slid his hand into mine.

"Anne," he said softly, "please marry me. Let me take care of you and help you have the joy-filled life you deserve. You needn't grind yourself down on that farm. Let me come and live there as your husband and share your load."

Nate's offer was wholly unexpected, but not unwelcome. There was a glimmer of protest in me—a part that noticed Nate's proposal was more about rescuing me than loving me. But before the protest could fully lodge itself in my heart, I reminded myself that I would become Mrs. Nathaniel Wilkins for that very reason—for protection and relief, and not for passion at all.

"Yes, Nate." I squeezed his hand. "I will."

Nate Wilkins planted a gentle kiss on my cheek, and in my heart I wished Jonas Blake farewell for good.

Sometimes I felt guilty for agreeing to marry Nate. He was assuredly a convenient solution to our problem, and perhaps in more carefree years I could have loved him. I dared not think of how my heart would fare had I never met Jonas. He had awakened a streak of courage and light in my heart two years ago. The time of war and sadness extinguished it, and I couldn't imagine that feeling being resurrected by another young man. As it was, I felt kindly toward Nate, was always contented by his attention, and did not think badly on our coming years as man and wife.

Nate's father was willing to let him live with us on Summerton farm for a time, but when the war ended and life was ordinary once more, he expected Nate to return and take over the Wilkins family farm. I dared not ask when that would be, or if Tom and Betsy could join us. It was all I could do to survive each day.

Our wedding date was set for the fall, for reasons not understood by me. Even in these times of war, Nate's industrious mother, Minnie, was set on me having wedding clothes and all the usual matrimonial trappings—and as I was motherless, she took it upon herself to see to these duties.

"It will take at least three months to gather your trousseau—and then you may marry," she said. Sometime in September—well after Norrington's deadline of producing a worthwhile man to run our farm.

Betsy stared at me intently.

"Anne? Do you think you could rush your wedding to Nate?" she repeated.

If Norrington forced our land from us before my wedding, we would be homeless. The loss of our beloved farm, so soon after watching our parents die, would be devastating. There would be very little left of me to marry Nate.

"I … I don't know," I stammered, my usual poise unraveling. "Mrs. Wilkins said she wants me to have clothes."

"Clothes." Betsy sniffed bitterly. "Our home is at stake, Anne. Hardly time to flounder about looking at new frocks."

My temper flared, but Betsy was in no humor to discuss my wardrobe; she was the one groomed to marry early, not me. Although, looking back, this wasn't the first time my hand had been sought—surely for Betsy that must sting. I soothed my hackles and turned my mind back to the matter at hand.

"I must go to Sussex and see if I can do something," I said, mainly to have a task to do. After all, it was the last Monday in May—it should be Court Day. I strode quickly toward the door, removing my apron and hanging it on the hook by the stove. There must be somebody in authority with whom I could share my troubles.

Sussex County had a magistrate, ten miles away in Sussex Village. Township business was at the mercy of the county court, which was largely comprised of farmers—not lawmakers—and only met once per month, and then it was on the green of the courthouse, in Sussex itself. We had no local law to speak of, particularly with so many men away from their homes.

Perhaps in Sussex Village I could find the magistrate and tell him my story, and in turn, receive some aid. After all, I could be silver-tongued when it suited me ... although the mood to please had left me long ago.

Tom followed me to the door, while Betsy cleared the tea things. He leaned down and spoke in my ear.

"Anne, what about the potatoes? We have to plant them this week for us to have a crop. They can't plant themselves, and you know Betsy and I ... " he trailed off, shaking his limp arm in apology.

Too much too fret about, I thought. *Oh, if I were a man! I would wring Norrington's plump neck!*

Instead, I hugged Tom's skinny one.

"I love you, brother," I said resolutely. "You help me more than you can know."

He shrugged from my embrace, embarrassed and unconvinced.

"I'll ride with you," was all he said.

IN WHICH I AM
TAKEN ABACK

JUNE 1775

That April saw the first major fighting in the disagreement with the British. Folks in Abbingdon continued their work as usual, putting their hands to the plow and praying that the war would stay in Massachusetts. The anti-British fervor was widespread in the cities, and though there was talk of it in the village sometimes, the people of our town mostly kept quiet. Maybe they thought that if they didn't mention it, the war would stay away. But it would not.

Planting day arrived early that year. We had a premature spring—the frost scared away in early May. For two weeks, Father and his hands were out in full force, plowing, planting, repeat. The job of feeding and watering the eight tired and hungry men fell to Betsy and Mother and me. Endless hours were spent in the kitchen, kneading bread dough, slicing ham and potatoes, and churning butter. My arms burned all day, and I fell into bed exhausted every night. The only consolation was taking that tray of biscuits to Jonas each day.

Since the day I slipped on the ice, something had shifted between us. Jonas, it seemed, had lost interest in me. His manners were more deferential, his gaze respectful. At first, I was angry that I lost my friend, that our old ways of bantering were apparently over. As the winter warmed into spring, I tried countless times to goad him into conversation, but was respectfully denied each time. A slight nod of his head, a shifting of his gaze, but never would he engage me in dialogue. I wondered what I had done. Recalling that day in the barn, I knew that my embarrassment at his laughter had unleashed my pride—it was disconcerting that he had such an obvious effect on me. Those months were filled with girlish worry and anxiety over Jonas. Each day I hoped he would behave like the old days, and each day I was disappointed.

But as summer arrived, something replaced our effortless friendship.

The first day of June dawned unseasonably warm, and that meant taking the bedclothes outside and beating them. I knew what was in store for my day when my eyes opened at first light. The sun was just peeking over the horizon, but already the day was shining. The sun would be blinding within hours. I quickly closed my eyes again.

"No, no, no, no," I muttered, waking Betsy up with my mumblings. They were to no avail. My mother hollered at me shrilly up the stairs.

"Anne! Anne! Get up, strip the beds, and get those quilts down to the tree for beating!"

This was my least favorite job. I didn't mind hard work and was not one to shirk my duties. Helping my mother was important to me. It's just that I was young, my mind prone to wander, and beating blankets was such monotonous work. One had to stand by the oak tree and hit the heavy rugs and quilts countless times with the mallet, the mind growing number with each stroke.

"No, not beating!" I wailed.

"Ha, ha, you have to beat today," Betsy gloated, sitting up and tossing her long, blonde braid over her shoulder. "I'll just be churning some butter today, or maybe some mending."

"Oh, hush, you. At least I'll get to be outside."

"Sure, with all those stinky farmhands." Her nose turned up as she spoke. "Disgusting."

The mention of the farmhands brought that infernal blush to my cheeks and a burning in my stomach, so I quickly turned my back to

Betsy and leaped out of bed. I dressed speedily, trying to choose my least dowdy work dress and endeavoring to leave my bonnet behind.

I spent the next hour pulling linens from all of the closets and rolling rugs from the bedroom floors. By the time I entered the kitchen, arms full of quilts, my mother had already pulled the rugs from the parlor and the sitting room. Mother took the blankets from me and ushered me to the table, where a slice of bread and a cup of tea awaited me. During the summer, my father was up so early that we didn't attempt to share the morning meal with him.

"Anne," my mother scolded, "put your bonnet on. The sun is bright out there. You don't want freckles, do you?" She shook her head and mumbled to herself, something about young girls and wretched skin.

I dawdled over my tea and bread, my reluctance to beat the rugs outweighing my desire to catch a glimpse of Jonas. Really, he was probably way out in the north pasture with my father already and wouldn't be around.

And if he was, would he talk to me? Would he just nod at me politely and say, "Miss Anne," with that undefined something lying dormant beneath his demeanor? Such a reaction would surely drive me mad!

"Anne," my mother snapped, "finish your tea. Jonas will be up here in a minute to help you take the linens outside."

I nearly fell into my cup. My stomach churned into a hard knot, and my face was on fire. My bite of bread balled up in my throat. My mouth suddenly was dry as a desert—but I drained the remainder of my now-tepid tea and pushed myself back from the table. I somehow managed with my wobbly limbs to gather the quilts and turn toward the door. My mother grasped my shoulders roughly, fixing my bonnet on my head.

"Crazy, stubborn, child," she muttered to herself as she tied my bonnet strings and opened the door, giving my shoulder a gentle shove.

I stumbled over the grass to the large oak tree southeast of our house. It was on the far side of the barn, hidden from the kitchen window. This was the advantage to the dreaded task of beating—I could dawdle all I liked during my task and my mother couldn't see. If I hadn't been so flustered that morning, I would have thought to retrieve my latest novel from under my mattress and take some reading time under the shelter of the foliage.

As I approached the grand old oak, I spotted Jonas leaning against it. Despite the fact that he'd already been working for hours, he still looked clean and fresh, his sandy brown hair pulled into a neat queue (as was the fashion of patriots), and his clothes relatively clean. I took a deep breath, willed myself to calm down, not to blush, and not to say anything dull.

A twig snapped under my feet; he looked up. When he saw me, he rushed toward me and took the linens from me. His hands brushed my arms as he removed my load, and if my arms could have blushed, they would have shown telltale red-hot streaks where the quilts left them.

"Good morning, Miss Anne," Jonas said. His voice was quiet, polite. Were his eyes twinkling?

"Good morning, Mr. Blake," I responded primly.

He draped the pile of quilts over a low branch, choosing one from the group. I took one corner from him, and together we hung it over the highest branch. Silence dominated our task. Jonas looked completely at ease, comfortable, not nervous at all, as I was. I looked around helplessly for the mallet we used to beat the linens.

"I don't have a mallet," I murmured.

So much for not saying anything dull.

"Oh, I'll get it." He lithely ran to the barn, leaving me a blissful moment to calm my nerves. Oddly enough, the first thing I thought to do was cast a glance toward the house to see if my mother was out on the stoop watching me. She wasn't there. I stood motionless until Jonas returned.

"Here you go." He handed me the mallet.

"Thank you, Mr. Blake." I sighed, already disappointed that my stolen moment with him was about to end. Trying to forget he was there, I lifted the mallet and began to beat the quilt with fierce anger and disappointment. Dust from last October poured out and floated up into the sky, the morning breeze lifting it up to the top of the ancient tree. I didn't think about my spying mother, or if Jonas had left for the fields; I just continued to beat that silly quilt into oblivion.

Suddenly, Jonas reminded me he was there.

"Anne," he said quietly, stopping me in my tracks at the use of my first name, "maybe you should go easy on that quilt. You're beating a hole in it. Move around to the other side."

How I managed to move my legs to the other side of the quilt, I'm not entirely sure, but I walked to where he was standing and began to beat the quilt again. It felt like my arms were moving through mud, as if my body, as well as time, had slowed down. Was Jonas still there? Why didn't he leave? My eyes remained trained on the suspended quilt as I swung the mallet again and again.

I lifted up the mallet to swing, and this time my arm stayed back behind me. Jonas's hand encircled my wrist as he took the mallet and turned me toward him. The calm demeanor had left him, and his eyes were like shining fire. From the corner of my eye, I noted that the quilt shielded us from view for miles around. Father and the hands were at the field on the other side of the barn. Mother was most likely busy in the kitchen and well out of sight.

We were completely alone.

My hand was still in his.

"Anne," he said quietly.

"Mr. Blake," I answered, not pulling my hand away. Actually, I was willing myself not to tremble, but it was hard going. There was an air of expectation hanging between us, the air charged with electricity.

And then it was gone. "You are beating a hole in that poor quilt. Why don't you let me take a turn?"

My breath whooshed from my chest in disappointment. Feeling curiously foiled, as if a moment had been stolen from me, I tipped my chin in a defiant little nod. Yanking my hand from his, I stepped away from him, seating myself in the warm grass and reclining onto my back, for staring at the sky was far better than staring stupidly at Jonas.

After carefully folding the first quilt and laying it next to me, Jonas picked a new quilt from the pile and hung it over the branch. He retrieved the mallet and beat the quilt slowly and methodically, almost lulling me to sleep.

However, sleep was not part of Jonas's immediate plan. As soon as I was comfortable he glanced my way.

"Aren't we going to talk, Anne?"

"Talk?"

"Of course." He shot me a smile from his post by the tree. "We used to talk all the time."

"Yes, before you grew so stuffy."

He laughed at that, throwing his head back and momentarily losing his rhythmic swinging. "Stuffy? Is that it?"

I glared mulishly. "As you say."

"I suppose I may have appeared so to you."

"Well, yes. All of this 'Miss Anne' nonsense, all bowing and politeness, none of the bright, lively Jonas I once knew."

He continued to beat the quilt, his back to me, in even, steady strokes. The work shirt he wore was surely white once, but was now faded to a sun-worn tan. Even so, his linen waistcoat was neat and clean, if not slightly threadbare. I shook my head in pity—Jonas was so fine he should be wearing the smartest clothes in Virginia.

His steady voice interrupted my musings about his wardrobe.

"By your calculations, I have certainly become stuffy. It's no wonder you are sore with me."

"I? Sore? *I* am not sore, Jonas."

He stopped beating and swung his head over to me, shooting me a knowing look that was almost condescending. Truth be told, I didn't quite care for it.

"To be sure, you are, Anne."

I looked away into the fields. Our pastures were beautiful, lush, green ... a summertime paradise. Summerton Farm was magnificent, and I was Anne Summerton. Why should I hide my thoughts and feelings, like hiding my face behind my ridiculous bonnet? Pride for my family and my farm bred courage inside me, and I found my voice. I leaped to my feet and stood up squarely in Jonas's face, closer to him than I'd ever dare drawn, fixing him with an even stare.

"Well, Jonas, we *were* once friends. But you have grown cold and distant, never speaking to me. So, yes, I suppose I am sore!"

There was a battle going on for control of my stomach—the knot of nerves was fighting valiantly against the courage that bubbled there. I paused, awaiting his anger, his laughter, his derision. But he surprised me by nodding seriously.

"Yes, Anne, we were friends. But that time is past. We can't be friends anymore."

The battle was over—the knot of nerves prevailed. My stomach seemed to drop down, down, out of my body into the ground beneath me. An empty hole stood in its place. My life as I knew it, flippant girl of fifteen that I was, was barren without the sparkling presence that was Jonas. I couldn't prevent the wicked tear that sprung from my eye and careened down my cheek.

"Can't?" I whispered, betrayed by my loss of valor. Jonas's warm finger retrieved my tear as he shook his head.

"No."

"Why?"

Jonas's response was concise, delivered with a casual shrug.

"Because I believe I love you."

"You love me? *Me?*"

Jonas nodded slowly, his excitement and feeling barely contained.

"I do, Anne, honest. I can't stop thinking about you."

"Could have fooled me," I said. My old hurt of the past month, of him ignoring me, flared up again even in the face of his astounding declaration. "You've barely noticed me since March. It's been plain awful without your friendship."

Jonas took my hand and bored his blue eyes into mine. The stare was so deep, so intense, that it rendered me speechless.

"Once I knew how I felt, I couldn't treat you like a sister anymore. Our relationship had to be different. Believe me, Anne, it has been quite difficult to not talk with you as we once did. I wish to talk to you all the time! But God requires me to treat my love with honor. I distanced myself to show you that I honored you."

I should have been deeply moved by his words and his gallant intentions, but I was only fifteen, and at that age the attention is much more satisfying.

"Well, you should have said something."

Jonas's serious demeanor cracked, and he chuckled and lifted a hand to stroke my cheek. "Sweet Anne," he said. "I'm going to marry you."

"Marry me?" I whispered, stepping closer to him until our faces were inches apart. "Are you sure?"

"Yes." Jonas nodded. "Will you?"

I paused and thought for a moment. Recalling the painful absence of his friendship, I thought that I could spend a forever or more with him if that's what he wanted.

I smiled. "Well, sure, Jonas."

He laughed and leaned away from me, but kept hold of my hand.

"Don't you want to kiss me?" I asked.

The answer was swift, assured, and unequivocal. "No, ma'am. Not until we are married."

I sighed.

He laughed, though I couldn't say what was funny.

"You're young yet," he said with a grin, "but I had to claim you while I had the chance. And Anne, we probably should wait a time, a year, maybe, before we ask your father."

"A *year?*" My heart nearly fell again. "That's a long time to keep a secret."

But keep it we did.

IN WHICH I
MAKE A SCENE

SUSSEX, MAY, 1777

Sussex County had no proper courthouse.

We were not a largely populated county, nor did we have any influential cities the likes of Richmond or Williamsburg. Nay, the seat of Sussex County—deemed Sussex in a fit of originality—was nearly as small a village as Abbingdon. In fact, it was quite a simple matter for Tom and I to wind our way to the center of town and to locate the worn, red brick building that was currently housing the court day proceedings.

Court Day was usually held once per month. Although the Commonwealth had an organized court system, the House of Burgesses found that many of the everyday legal issues common in the small villages could be eradicated if the county sheriff could spend one day per month simply hearing the questions and grievances of the county's residents. In effect, Court Day was a holdover from Medieval England, and although the American colonies were trying to break free from England at the moment, one was forced to admit that some of the English traditions we'd adopted were worthwhile endeavors.

The red brick edifice was easy to identify by the dozens of people pouring out of its door. Every level of society was represented in that angry, impatient swarm: the wealthy landowner, the tradesman, the freed slave, the indentured servant, and even a few plain farm owners like Tom and me.

To say I was reluctant to insert myself into this throng was an understatement. Somehow I felt that the petty bickering of my fellow townspeople—most likely disputes over land boundaries or stolen livestock—were inconsequential in comparison with what was transpiring in my own town, indeed, on my own farm. And yet, I had no recourse but to place myself in the end of the queue and await my turn to see the magistrate.

The man in front of me was obviously a farmer as well—the scent of alfalfa and manure was quite familiar to me, and the hen tucked under his arm further confirmed my assessment. From his mouth protruded a piece of hay, which poked me in the nose as he swung his face around to glance at us.

"Mornin,'" he said nodding at Tom and me congenially.

We returned the gesture, and he looked his chicken in the eyes.

"Not much longer, Mrs. Jenkins," he whispered, stroking her tail feathers, "and we'll sort this business out."

Tom's eyes met mine in a delightful mix of disbelief and unconcealed amusement. He leaned toward my ear.

"I am quite eager to see how his case turns out, Anne. Can we go in with him and listen?"

"Oh, hush, Tom!" I elbowed him, chuckling myself. Unfortunately, Mrs. Jenkins's owner overheard our snickering and shot us a withering look.

"Mrs. Jenkins is quite a famous Bantam up Carlton way," he informed us.

Tom nodded seriously. "It's quite easy to see why, sir. She is obviously a high quality ... chicken."

I drew a deep breath to suppress my giggle until the man turned his back to us again, but I was unsuccessful. Believing he found a true compatriot in his devotion to chickens, the man made himself comfortable next to Tom, acquainting him with all manners of chicken-lore, and enumerated Mrs. Jenkins's many accomplishments. Tom matched the man comment-for-question, and all in all was an exceptional conversation partner. For my part, I was amazed at how knowledgeable Tom seemed to be about the Bantam breed. It was not a short conversation, and in the end I had to smother my giggles in a cough.

My fits drew the man's attention away from Tom and his hen. He jerked his thumb at me and addressed Tom. "Is your wife sick? I don't want Mrs. Jenkins taking ill."

Tom shook his head quickly. "She's not my wife, sir. This here is my sister."

The man's eyes widened. "Your sister? Don't you all have a father?"

"Our father is taken abed," I answered. My mirth dissipated as quickly as it arose.

"So you're the man of the house, then?" the man asked Tom, who glanced at me uncomfortably.

That particular issue turned out to be quite important, and one that Tom and I had not considered.

Two hours in the queue finally yielded us our turn in front of the magistrate. During that time we became very well informed on just how dramatic a court day could be. The magistrate would first hear the complaints of the witness. Often the person being complained against was present and would begin shouting in protest at the previous witness's account of the story. Many of the complaints in front of the judge ended in a yelling match, and more than one resulted in fisticuffs.

Watching such poorly composed members of the community lent me a measure of confidence. When Tom and I approached the magistrate, we would be eloquent and calm, with a firm command of our emotions, and surely the judge would be more disposed to help us with such a display of the facts.

"Next!" The magistrate's firm and resounding call startled us into action.

As we approached him we passed Mrs. Jenkins and her owner, who looked desperately upset. However, Tom and I were now too anxious to comment on what might have been Mrs. Jenkins's fate, as we entered the judge's presence.

The area itself was actually quite small, just a wood-paneled room with a small, east-facing window. A diminutive desk sat in its center, flanked by two tall bookcases. The judge bore the stamp of the aristocrat—high forehead, arched brows, and supremely bored disposition. He did not wear a wig; quite early in the conflict with the British, true patriots sacrificed that fashion in exchange for real ponytails to lend solidarity to their cause. However, even wigless, his hair was carefully coiffed, his patriot's ponytail meticulously curled in a manner befitting his office.

He glanced at us with barely concealed disdain. "Can I help you?"

"Yes, sir," I began. "We live in Abbingdon, see, and..."

"Not you," he interrupted, swinging his glance to Tom. "You, tell me your business."

Tom flicked his eyes at me, then back at the magistrate. "Sir, we're from Abbingdon, and we're having trouble with this man in town. You see, he..."

"Are you two married?"

"No," Tom answered. "We're brother and sister."

The man sighed in exasperation. "I need to hear the complaint from the head of household. Who is the head of household? Do you not have a father who can represent your case?"

"Our father is taken abed. He is ill," I cried, quite tired of his incessant bullying.

"You will not speak unless spoken to, miss," he responded, staring down his nose at me before addressing Tom once more. "So with your father to his bed, who is handling the household business?"

Tom glanced at me. "My sister here is handling most of the work, sir." I saw his eyes pass reluctantly over his useless arm and foot.

Not for the first time, I felt a squeeze of pity for my admirable brother.

The judge, who must have noticed Tom's limp as we entered the room, had the good breeding not to needle Tom about his limbs. He turned his eyes to me.

"And are you married?"

I shook my head. The judge looked me over thoroughly, his eyes taking in my dress (not my best), my hands (clean, but callused and worn), my hair (hadn't the time to fix it properly), and finally my face (set in stubborn determination).

"It's quite improper for you to be the sole proprietor of your family's farm, Miss … ?"

"Summerton. My name is Anne Summerton."

"Ah, yes." He nodded. "Quite. Well, as I say, I suggest you marry as soon as you may, miss, because a young, unmarried woman is unlikely to receive any attention from the law in these times."

"Excuse me, sir, but isn't that quite unfair?"

He shrugged. "Unfair? I don't know whether it's unfair, miss, but it *is*. Any complaint you file today will be summarily"—he paused "overlooked, without a head-of-household's evidence."

I sighed, beyond exasperated at this infuriating turn of affairs.

"And who would qualify as a head-of-household?"

"Your father or your husband."

"So if I was to be dishonest and tell you that Thomas here was my husband, you would happily listen to my complaint and it would not be—as you say—overlooked?" My tone was dangerously bordering on mocking, I knew, but my anger was boiling and just barely held at bay.

The judge met my livid gaze, boring into my eyes with his own. He would not take my sass, I could see. A man of his ilk would sooner toss me straight out of this office than be verbally berated by an unmarried young woman.

"That is true," he said, his voice taking on a malicious edge, "but then...I am already acquainted with the fact that he is your brother."

I stood abruptly, quickly discerning that we would find no help here. "Come, Thomas," I said, "let us ride to Williamsburg."

There was the barest flicker of something in the judge's eyes—not quite fear—it was more akin to irritation.

"Yes, you go ahead and do that, Miss Summerton. Just mind you take a husband on the journey there."

Storming from the office, I burst through the doors to the street in a rush of blind rage. A lengthy queue of people was still assembled at the building's door—a true mingling of society, half of which would not be served by the laws of our country.

"I wonder," I shouted at the top of my voice, "if Mr. Jefferson's inalienable rights are reserved for women, as well?"

"Anne, hush!" Thomas urged me, taking my arm and attempting to lead me away from the center of town.

"Life, liberty and the pursuit of happiness all sound delightful...if you're a *man!*" I continued to shout. "Tell me, Mr. Jefferson, do you think us ladies unworthy of such things?"

The people in line expressed a motley mix of reactions to my outbursts; some were embarrassed for me, some angered, and a few—I garnered as Tom finally succeeded in escorting me to my horse—just a few, were grinning in open support.

Enough. A few supporters were quite enough—for today.

IN WHICH A
BARN IS RAISED

SUMMERTON FARMS, AUGUST 1775

Not even war against the British could keep my father from the building of the barn. He was pleased that there was even a need for such a thing, and that need, whether merely perceived or perfectly valid, puffed him up with immensely amusing pride.

The old barn, which housed our few horses and farm equipment, was found to be rotting in its roof beams and must come down. Father never liked the location of that barn anyway. The slight downward slope leading from our house to the barn tended to collect water, and therefore, ice; it made for a slippery walk out there several times a day. I could personally attest to its dangers. So, Father had decided, the new barn would be on the north side of the house, on an altogether level plain.

"We'll need to have a barn raising," he said gruffly to Mother during afternoon tea. His manners did naught to fool any of us. The rest of the Summertons were well aware that a barn raising was one of Father's favorite community events.

It was typical in the rural areas to elevate the construction of a new barn to a village affair. Of course, the owner of the barn and his hands would do all of the preparation work well in advance: preparing the lumber, assembling the frames, and doweling the beams before the frames could be erected. However, the real fun would begin when the local farmers from miles around would come with *their* farmhands and *their* families to assist in transforming those skeletal frames into a serviceable building. Of course, after all of the work was done, there would be a great need for a roasted pig, several rounds of ale, music, dancing, and tall-tale telling. But who could argue with these activities, especially when such hard labor had been performed and such an excellent goal achieved?

When we were alone and out of Mother and Father's earshot, Tom and I wondered if Father didn't want a new barn just to have an excuse for some wild festivities. But we would never say such a thing to another living soul. Certainly not to Betsy, whose tongue would waggle and tell Father our opinion.

For me, to have the opportunity to interact with Jonas was reason enough to build a new barn, needlessly or no.

As morning dawned on August fifteenth, it became evident that the barn raising would not entirely be all pleasure and gaiety. My mother's resounding shout from the kitchen, meant to rouse Betsy and me from our slumbers, told this tale well enough.

"Girls! If we are to feed the entire community this evening, I am going to need some assistance straight away!"

Rolling out of bed and quickly donning work frocks, Betsy and I trudged downstairs to receive the litany of chores required before the guests would arrive at two o'clock.

"Potatoes? I don't *want* to peel potatoes!" Betsy complained. "They leave my hands all starchy and dry. Anne, you don't care as much for your appearance—will you not peel the potatoes? I will trade a task with you."

"Betsy, my own tasks include cleaning the yard—where we will set the food tables—airing out the tablecloths, creating extra space in the stables for the horses…" I allowed my voice to trail away with studied nonchalance.

Betsy turned up her nose. "*Outside* chores." She sniffed. "Very well. I will need to soak my hands in vinegar to soften them before this afternoon."

Smiling to myself, I gleefully bounded out of the kitchen door into the wide yard at the southern end of our farmhouse. An expansive grassy area, perfect for picnicking, boasted several large oak trees for shade. To be sure, I was enamored with my home, but even an unbiased eye would have to admit to the picturesque beauty of such a place.

My morning was busily spent clearing the area of stray limbs and rocks in an attempt to widen the clearing so Father and the hands could erect tables on which to lay the food. The guests would be bringing their own quilts or blankets for picnic seating. The weather was beautiful—the air warm and smelling of summer. It was to be a sublime evening.

There was no sign of Jonas or the other hands that day. My father kept them all quite busy. He even had Tom at the barn site with them, kicking the joints in the frames to assure their security. My lively brother had caught the barn fever, the same as the others.

Betsy and I barely had time to wash and change our frocks before the carriages started arriving. Our closest friends, the Hudgins, were among the first families to turn their carriage onto our lane. The Wilkinses, the Brownes, and the Hardwickes followed. My good friend, Mary Hudgins, bounded from her carriage and approached me with a girlish squeal (and a new novel), whereby I ceased to notice who else was arriving. Mary and I found a pleasant seat in the lowest branch of an oak tree near the eating area and began to chatter with gay abandon.

The actual raising of the barn took several hours and garnered little attention from us. Even Betsy, who longed to impress some of the more genteel young men from Abbingdon—enough to don her lavender cambric gown with the velvet stomacher—quickly lost interest in the more masculine proceedings of the event. As for my costume, I chose one of my simplest muslin dresses in light blue, for I knew spending time outdoors required a sturdier cloth.

Mary, Betsy, and I sidled over to the barn site near dusk, after Tom informed us that there was finally something worth looking at. We were pleased to see the four walls completely framed and the roofline nearly complete. Soon, only the siding would remain. A few of the farm hands had already left the barn to light the bonfire. The pig, which had been roasting since the previous evening, was completely cooked and nearly ready to eat—but for appearance's sake, Father would suspend the meat above the bonfire on the iron grate, where the guests could serve themselves the cut of their choice.

I inhaled deeply, breathing in the heady scent of a summer fire, when we heard a shout from the roof of the new barn.

"Whoa! Careful, down there!"

One of the hands had dropped his hammer and bucket of nails from his perch on the barn's roof. They fell harmlessly to the ground where nobody stood, but the accident was close enough to induce Mary and me to take a few steps back away from the danger. We could hear Tom and Edward Hudgins whooping in laughter at the poor man's mistake, and from his own perch on the roof, Father spoke sternly in low tones.

"Miss Anne?"

A familiar voice to my left caused a slight increase in my body temperature. After a second to cool my nerves, I turned to face Jonas. "Yes, Mr. Blake?"

He stood several inches away from me, the picture of propriety, although he had removed his coat for the hard labor. There was sawdust littering his sandy-brown hair, which was quickly coming loose from its ponytail. His blue eyes were trained on me, and though they were warm with emotion, I could also detect a note of wariness there.

"I believe it would be much safer if you ladies were seated over there." He gestured to a clump of maple trees several yards away from the barn—too far away to be beamed on the head by cascading tools.

I arched an eyebrow. "Mr. Blake, surely we are perfectly safe at this distance from the barn. There are dozens of people *here,* and there are no people over *there*." I waved my arms about to emphasize my point.

Jonas pursed his lips in barely contained disapproval. "It only requires one person too near the barn to be involved in an accident, Miss Anne." His tone had quickly transformed from subservient farmhand proper to worried, frustrated betrothed.

Emboldened by my audience and reluctant to leave the lively crowd merely for my safety's sake, I spoke my next words with condescending mischief.

"Mr. Blake, why are you not instructing all of the spectators to move away to their safety? Are the three of us ladies somehow exceptional?" I willed him with my eyes to smile, be amused at my youthful sauciness, but I was disappointed.

His eyes flared with exasperation. "Miss Anne, I believe your father would appreciate my intervention in the matter of his daughter's safety... no offense intended for Miss Hudgins."

Mary barely noticed him. "Oh, no offense taken, Jonas," she quipped, her eyes eagerly scanning the crowd. "Betsy! I spy my brother at the other end of the barn."

Betsy was examining her hands to gauge if her vinegar bath had been successful. She was not impressed. "Yes, yes, Mary. Edward is here every day."

"No, Betsy. I speak of my *other* brother. He must have ridden home from Williamsburg this weekend. Come and say hello?" she taunted, never able to find a more willing accomplice than my sister.

Betsy affected an air of pretty gentility and followed Mary away in search of greener pastures.

Jonas and I were left alone, and without my audience, my bravado fled.

"Shall I go sit at the maples?" I asked.

Bowing shortly at the neck, he cast me a glance replete with surrender and affection. "As you wish, Miss Anne. I believe the best view of the barn is afforded from that direction. May I escort you?"

I took his proffered arm with a grin. "Yes, Mr. Blake. I believe you may."

After another hour of hard work, amid shouts of encouragement from the men aground and yawns of boredom from the ladies, Father's new barn was finally erected in all of its glory.

My father alighted on the ground from his position on the roof, brushed off his hands, and made an announcement to the people gathered there. "Friends from Abbingdon and all about, I am so pleased to have you all here at my home. I thank you for your hard work and the wide show of Christian charity that you would come to assist me in this endeavor. Who says we are not Americans?"

This last elicited a hearty whoop from the crowd, for since the war began, Father's position as a Patriot had been made clear.

"I invite you all to join us for roasted pig and ale by the bonfire. And those of you who brought your instruments and your talents, I beseech you to warm them up so these young people can dance!"

There was a general din of good cheer emanating from the crowd as we made our way over to the fire. I watched my father in admiration as he led our friends to the feast. He was tall and strong, radiating power, influence, and goodness. His principals were his ready guides in all things, from his farm to his family. Richard Summerton was an inspiration to the people who knew him and had the good fortune to work with him.

The feast was prettily displayed beneath the oak trees. The largest of the fires was housing the carcass of our supper, and several smaller fires were set about the area to provide light and warmth. Although it was August, once the sun disappeared, the air did tend to turn cool. Each table was laid with a bounty of vegetables and fruit from our own harvest and from the neighboring farms that had contributed their wares. Betsy, Mary, and I ate until we were beyond stuffed—not an easy task when one is attempting to appear dainty before the young men in the crowd.

At length the musicians fulfilled Father's wishes with some rousing music, which in turn encouraged several couples to begin twirling amongst the bonfires. A couple of the farmhands shyly sidled up to Betsy and asked her to dance, only to be soundly rejected. I sighed in disappointment as I surveyed the scene—Jonas would never ask me to dance, not in front of the entire village. For the other farmhands and Betsy, it was mere fun. For us, it was too near the truth.

And so it was with regret that I tapped my foot on the grass, wishing to dance but knowing my preferred partner would keep his seat across the clearing—laughing with the other farmhands and occasionally casting a wistful glance my way. Imagine my surprise when Nathaniel, the eldest son of the Wilkins family who lived on the north road between Abbingdon and Carlton, approached me shyly.

"Care to dance, Miss Summerton?" Nathaniel stood before me, hand outstretched with a charming smile.

I knew Nate but little. Our families were slightly acquainted at church, but we had never shared conversation beyond the prosaic talk of the weather, crops, or animals.

"Oh," I stammered, glancing across the fire at Jonas, who was steeped in conversation with my brother, "I … "

"Come, Anne! I must have you dance!" My father appeared from behind me, slapping my back and applying a gentle shove. "Are you afraid you and Wilkins haven't had a proper introduction? Nate, allow me to present Anne, my younger daughter. Anne, this fine young man is Nate Wilkins."

Nate inclined his head slightly, his brown eyes twinkling. "Charmed, Miss Anne."

I had no recourse but to bob a small curtsey in return. "How do you do, Mr. Wilkins?"

"Excellent!" My father boomed, and it dawned on me he had taken an abundance of ale. "That's settled, then. Off you go, young people!"

The proprieties dispensed with, Nate pulled me by the hand to the circle of twirling couples and set about joining the dance. I had to admit, it was as much pleasure as I'd expected it to be, only the partner was wrong.

On our second twirl around the fire, I glanced up and noticed Jonas watching us. He did not look angry, only contemplative. I managed to fix him with a special smile, and it found its mark. On our next turn in his direction, he grinned at me affectionately.

The dancing and merry making continued throughout the whole of the evening. The time drew near to midnight when the crowd began to disperse. Jonas managed to steal me away to the barn for a few moments to explain the finer points of engineering and construction, none of which I applied myself to—being much too interested in holding his hand and trying to cultivate romance.

"So it really is an abundance of work," Jonas was saying, pointing to the joists where the beams were attached. "Much has to be done before the actual day of assembling."

"Oh, I am aware of that," I said dryly, recalling the many months of Father urging the farmhands to work harder. The din of felling trees and Father's shouts had been my constant companions the whole of the summer.

Willing Jonas to pay attention to me rather than the barn, I squeezed his hand in mine. My fingers trailed up his bare forearm, admiring its fine form.

"Anne ... " Jonas said softly, his tone stern.

"Jonas!" I protested. "We are rarely unaccompanied. I beg you, let us enjoy it!"

He stared at me for an endless moment, sighing deeply. Cupping my face in his palm, he leaned toward me very slowly, so slowly I thought I would die from the anticipation. His head bent over mine, a movement that positively tied me in knots.

Is he actually going to kiss me? I closed my eyes and realized I was holding my breath and then opened them again. The agitation was rendering me senseless! His proximity was so agonizing I began to tremble.

Suddenly he halted his descent toward my mouth, standing upright and looking at me squarely. "Well, Anne, what are you doing?"

I stared in shocked disappointment. "Trembling," I blurted.

Jonas grinned in response.

"That was very unkind of you to deceive me so," I said.

Affronted, Jonas raised his eyebrows innocently. "I wasn't deceiving you, Anne. I really was considering kissing you—I just thought better of it."

"Huzzah for you."

Laughing, Jonas cupped my face again, swiftly leaning down and brushing his lips against mine. It lasted but a moment, while the contact itself practically sent my body into jitters.

"There you are," Jonas said with a self-satisfied smirk. "How was it?"

"Hasty," I grumbled, "but it's a start."

He laughed heartily, and the sound echoed throughout the barn in its empty newness.

"Did you enjoy your dance?" he asked, taking my elbow and steering me toward the open barn door.

My stomach clenched, anxious. "Do you refer to my dance this evening with Nate Wilkins?"

Jonas looked away from me to his boots crunching on the clean barn floor. "Is that his name?"

"Yes," I said quietly. "Mr. Wilkins and Father are friends. Did my dancing with him trouble you?"

I could feel him shrug next to me. "Only in that I wished I could be your partner in his stead. But, no, he did not make me envious."

My anxious breath exhaled. "Oh, Jonas, I'm pleased to hear that."

We stopped at the barn door, where Jonas raised my hand to his lips in a silent gesture of affection.

A flurry of activity sounded from outside. Alerted to the first round of carriages rattling down the lane, we hurried back to the scene of the party to bid our farewell to the departing guests.

As I drew near to my parents, I could overhear the tail end of a conversation they were having with a man I did not recognize. The firelight illuminated the man's face, and I realized he was William Norrington, a landowner from Carlton. We were not much acquainted with him.

"It's an impressive piece of land you have here, Summerton," he said.

"Indeed," Father responded, draping his arm around my shoulders. "Norrington, please meet my younger daughter, Anne."

I bobbed a silent curtsey, while Norrington took my hand and bowed over it formally. His features turned wolfish as he glanced up at me.

"Charmed," he said. An unconscious shudder rippled through me.

"Yes," he went on, turning about and surveying our farm with a distasteful air of envy. "I surely do like your property, Mr. Summerton. I surely do."

IN WHICH I MAKE
ANOTHER SCENE

ABBINGDON, JUNE 1777

Court Day was, admittedly, a disaster, but that did not prevent Tom from conceding to ride directly into Abbingdon the next day to locate someone of our acquaintance who could give us some valid advice.

Our horses were much under worked, due to our not having leisure time for riding. As this ride to town seemed urgent, our mounts caught our mood and started to stamp and whinny in their stalls. They were ready for a swift gallop.

I took my mare by the nose. "I'm sorry, girl. It's only three miles! Not nearly long enough for you to release your angst and feel the glorious wind. I'm so, so sorry." As I was stroking her mane, my eye caught the peg above her stall. Father's musket sat there still, untouched and unused for months now. For some wild and unexplainable reason, I took it down, feeling its weight and sensing its power. With Tom unable to shoot, Father had taught me how after Jonas left. I was seeking an outlet for my frustration, and it was a way for us to spend time together in a neutral activity.

Now a musket is not the easiest machine to manipulate. There are no less than thirteen separate actions involved in firing one of those wily things, what with the cartridge, the powder, the ball, ramming the ball, and cocking the blasted thing before one could even fire. Who I was planning to shoot, I couldn't say for sure, but the musket lent me both a feeling of protection and a tie to my father that instilled me with confidence.

Tom quirked an eyebrow at me when he saw me strap the musket onto my saddle, but said nothing. I believe he knew better.

We rode silently into town, our horses energetic. The three miles into the village passed quickly, as Tom and I were wrapped in our own thoughts, although I would bet our farm that Tom's mirrored my own. Worry, worry, and more worry—and dread that nobody had the strength to stand up to Will Norrington.

In the back of my mind, I faintly heard God encouraging me that he had enough strength, and more besides. I had not heard God's voice in some time now—I was prone to tuning it out. With the bitterness, worry, and frustration I was carrying, I had no room in my mind for the spirit of God. So it was a long forgotten experience to hear it now, but in my present weakness, he wore down my last reserve of stubbornness. It made my limbs tingle to hear him speak.

"Tom," I said, keen to share my lighthearted thought.

He was staring down, his hat pushed low over his eyes.

"I think God will find a way to get us out of this."

Tom, who was naturally more hopeful than I, grinned.

"Why, yes, Annie. I think he will, too."

Emboldened by God's voice and Tom's encouragement, I turned my mind back to my task. Looking at the bare facts, the situation boiled down thus: my father was not going to improve. He was in his bed, and there he would stay. Marrying Nate would improve my chances of keeping my farm running, but it was not a certainty. We could live at Summerton for a time, but after all, Nate had his own farm to run—and if forced to choose between my acres and his own, I knew which way his heart would go. My heart, which was afloat with hope a moment ago, sunk a level as I felt the truth descend upon my bones; the only way to keep my farm was to get rid of Will Norrington, or at least end his tyranny.

I could think of no one able to achieve such a task.

Abbingdon was a small village—just a main square with a dozen buildings: a feed store, a post, a general store, a millinery, a cobbler, and a few other necessities. Most of its residents lived in large farms on the outskirts—very few families actually lived in the village. Tom rode on to the general store, and I stayed put, wishing to drink in the sight of my peaceful village. My eyes swept across the sad and tired buildings of our town. They were in disrepair, in need of strong hands and able bodies. Women hurried their children across the street— they would go home to a small supper without their father tonight. The war had not literally touched our village—no battles fought here, no militia marched through, and no British soldiers quartered in our homes—but all the same, our townspeople were affected by it. The war reached us all.

A commotion stirred from the feed store and drew my attention. I heard scuffling, heavy boots banging old wooden planks. I heard shouting but couldn't pick out specific words. Suddenly the yelling reached a critical volume; the screams increased as the door to the feed store banged open, and men began streaming out. After the first crowd fled, another group of men exited the building—this time carrying a body covered in blood.

The sight filled me with full-bodied dread—a man was bleeding, after all. Something in me wanted to run for the doctor; something stronger urged me to stay. I had the strange sensation that I had to go and see this bloody tragedy for myself. There was simply no strength to look away; it wasn't in me. I leaped from my horse and tied her to a post, walking over to the bleeding man like someone possessed. Men were running past me, flying, shouting for someone to fetch the doctor. Nobody noticed me until I was a few feet away, and then Mr. Joseph, the owner of the feed store, looked up from the bloody man and saw me.

"Oh, Anne," he moaned. "Oh, I'm so sorry, my dear."

The bloody man was Nate Wilkins, my betrothed.

The world shattered around me. No other image is fitting. It literally felt as if the world detached somewhere above—like the sky and the heavens were joined by some slatternly running stitch that unraveled too soon and the entire world collapsed. Voices and screams were muted; the colors around me faded. Poor Nate, even his blood-soaked body drifted away as an amber fog surrounded me. I stumbled away, walking blindly away from the shouts and the scene of the horrible accident. The sounds dissipated behind me as I stood, stock-still, in the street until my brother found me.

"Anne? Anne?" Tom's frantic voice penetrated my daze.

No, no, Tom. Let me be.

And then I felt that voice of God again, which I hadn't heard in so long. It didn't say anything specific, so much as it beckoned me back to the lacerated world in which I lived, promising that something better was coming along. This time the stitching would hold. And although my ears were still out of practice, I was so much in need of something bigger than myself that I listened.

I turned to my brother reluctantly. Tom's face leaned toward mine, strained with worry. His eyes were dark and circled with purple. My body felt heavy with fatigue. I reached out and steadied myself against his shoulder.

"Tom," I whispered. "What happened to Nate?"

I could see him struggling with something as he chewed his lip and averted his eyes. Finally, he heaved a great sigh and squeezed my shoulders. "He's dead, Annie."

"Dead?" I suppose I had suspected as much, but to hear the word spoken out loud carried an evil with it that settled heavily in my frame. Dead was something serious and permanent, something I was disinclined to deal with. I squared my shoulders, leaning away from Tom and glancing about me for my mount.

"What are you doing, Anne?" Tom asked, his eyes wide with wary caution.

"Thomas, I must leave this place. Now."

He shook his head, grasping my wrist and fixing me with a look of stern gravity. "No, Anne, you can't. Nate is lying over there dead, and you are his intended. You don't just jump on your horse and trot away, Anne. You walk over there and pay your respects to the man that wished to marry you and care for you."

Pulling a deep breath into my lungs, I stared back at him. "Now?"

Tom's eyebrows knitted together, and I knew there would be no further discussion. "*Now.*"

My feet began their long, hard shuffle to the feed store, where Nate's body was propped up against the wooden post. The other spectators of the skirmish had long fled the scene. It seemed to me some interminable number of hours since I first saw his body. In all truth, only a few minutes had passed. Many other townspeople were about—some crying, others wringing their hands. There was no sign of Will Norrington or any of his men—for someone who claimed to be the best leader for Abbingdon, he sure made himself scarce when an actual tragedy was afoot. I swallowed that bitter pill for the umpteenth time and crept to the feed store, where Mr. Joseph was crouched, holding Nate's head against the wooden post.

I squatted down beside the motionless, limp form of my betrothed, lifting his hand to my own. His torso was bloodied up good and thorough, but his face was mostly clean, and I was pleased to see that it looked peaceful.

"I hope he's happy at home with you, Lord," I murmured, feeling the first flush of tears spill onto my cheeks. The extent of unfairness displayed before me could not be counted or listed. That nobody was there to take charge of the men responsible angered me further, until red clouded my last glimpse of Nate's calm face.

Wiping my cheeks clean of tears, I leaned forward and planted a kiss on Nate's smooth brow. "Sleep well, Nate," I whispered, standing up and brushing my skirts clean. There were more tears to be shed for Nate, but at that point in time, they were buried beneath a fury that

I was unable to contain. Nate was dead. I was no longer an engaged woman, but was destined to be a homeless spinster, living in a rented room in town with Tom and Betsy.

Over the next few hours, we received sketchy details about the fight that ensued in the feed store and ended with Nate's death. Mr. Joseph, the owner, told us that Norrington was standing in the doorway with Ben Cummings, shooting the breeze. Nate was keeping to himself as usual, minding his own business, when he overheard a comment that made even his tranquil blood boil.

"I've got my eye on that Summerton Farm. It's only a matter of time, lads."

Nate pricked up his ears, turning slightly toward the conversation as Norrington continued.

"And I've got my other eye on that Summerton girl."

"Which one? Betsy's the beauty in that house."

"True, true—but that Anne has spirit and fire, and I like that in a lass. Like I said, lads, it's only a matter of time."

Well, Nate could stand this talk no more. It pained my heart to think of it. He was a man of honor and courage, standing up to those brutes with no thought of saving his own skin.

"Excuse me, gentlemen, but that is my betrothed of whom you speak."

Norrington was incredulous and angry. "What did he say? Say that again!"

"I said, the young lady of spirit and fire is to be my wife. And I would appreciate it if you didn't talk about her in that way."

Norrington needed no further provocation. Punches began to fly—other men from the store jumped in to help Nate, and soon there was a massive melee. A dozen men were swinging at whoever was the closest. The fighting destroyed the store. Several men had broken bones, broken teeth, or bruised fists. Will pulled out his knife, but only Nate lost his life.

The entire town was shocked by Nate's death. Norrington was becoming too much like the law, it was true, but there hadn't been any killing yet. However, Nate's death pushed Norrington into a corner—he had to establish himself as the law of our town or be subject to a higher law. He refused to lose his control over our people and couldn't afford to give up his power and wealth, so he chose the latter.

Within hours of the fight, Norrington called the people together in front of the post office. He apologized for Nate's death, but absolved himself of the blame, citing overexcitement of the mob instead. "Remember the problem in Boston?" he asked. "How one man lost his nerve and the entire mob lost control?"

Nate's death was just such a problem that proved our village needed a strong leader. And as Norrington was the largest landowner and the wealthiest, he declared himself the king of Abbingdon.

I was standing at the back of the crowd as this drivel was being pushed onto the residents, my blood not yet cooled from the fury that had overtaken me hours ago. Nate's parents had long come for him, solemnly taking him home to Carlton where they would bury him in their family plot. I had been too ashamed to speak to them, but instead cowered behind Tom at the post office. When Norrington's voice boomed in the streets, I wandered out, only to hear such a speech as this.

I saw no reason, only rage. Quickly, I strode over to my horse, unstrapping the musket and flying through the thirteen steps required to get the blasted thing loaded. Nobody seemed to notice me stomping through the crowd. I just caught the tail end of Norrington's speech about law and order as I pushed myself to the front.

"…just goes to show that we need my sort of control here—leastways while the war is on—until the men get back, of course."

I shoved through the last of the residents, coming face-to-face with Norrington, musket raised to his nose.

"Norrington!" I screamed, exacting no level of control over the tone or volume of my voice.

Norrington's eyes widened in fear, which satisfied me. His hands immediately went up in a gesture of defeat. Ben and the others rushed to his side, but he quickly shook his head.

"Why, Miss Anne?" he stammered. "What is all this anger about?"

"Dare you ask?" I shrieked. "You come to my house and threaten me with these"—I spat in Ben Cummings's direction—"these villains. You threaten to take my house with my sick father abed upstairs." I paused to cock the hammer on my musket, eliciting a gasp from Norrington and his cohorts. "And then you allow my betrothed to be *murdered*," I bit the word out savagely, hearing with gratification the gasps of my fellow townspeople. "Yes, *murdered!* And you stand here and blame it on us? The *mob?* You are trying to control us and steal our town, Norrington, and there will be the devil to pay for it." At the last my voice had reached its highest peak. I jammed the end of the musket into Norrington's nose. "It ends now," I told him with deadly calm, my finger dancing on the trigger mechanism.

"Annie! Anne Summerton!" Tom's voice shot through the silence, and it covered me, a balm to my unbridled fury. Suddenly I gained my surroundings: Norrington's frightened face, the anger of Ben Cummings, the shock of the people behind me, and my hands on an instrument of death, ready and very willing to take another life today.

God, I thought, *I am about to kill this man.*

Tom reached me as quickly as he could, snatching the musket from me.

"Anne Summerton," he whispered, "just *what* are you doing?"

Ben Cummings lost no time. "Grab that girl! She almost killed Will Norrington!"

Shouts abounded in all directions—supportive shouts from Norrington's friends, protests from the locals, and nothing at all from me, still blind with shock at my own thoughtless actions.

"You'll do nothing of the sort," Tom shouted. "She's mad with grief over the loss of Nate Wilkins. You people leave her be."

And on cue, I collapsed onto Tom's chest, halfway from honest exhaustion, and halfway for dramatic effect necessary for the moment. Ben Cummings backed away—Norrington had not commanded him to take me, after all. From the approving murmurs and encouraging shouts, the whole of Abbingdon seemed to be on my side. Tom dragged me back to my horse, taking the musket from me roughly.

"We've got to flee this place," I muttered, mounting my horse and quickly spurring her south, directly out of town. Once we cleared the edge of Abbingdon proper, the terror of the day's events descended on me. I kicked the mare and let her fly the three miles to our farm, screaming my fury into the wind as we flew. I didn't look back to see if Tom followed, but I knew he was back there somewhere.

I was replacing my saddle on its hook when Tom limped into the barn. His face was stern, and I knew I had a verbal lashing coming to me. Sighing, I swung my eyes to his.

"I know, I know," I said. "I can't recall what came over me, Tom. I was like a girl possessed. It was … crazy, it was. I am very aware of it."

He said nothing—for he had other news to share.

"When you were in the street, before you … well, you recall," he began, eyes narrowed. "I was at the post, and I came upon Charlotte Blake."

I drew in a sharp breath, trying to inflate my chest, which had constricted at the mention of Jonas's sister.

"And how do she and Mrs. Blake fare?" My back was turned to Tom. If he noticed my distress, he wasn't showing it. Good lad.

"Oh, she's in the same kind of pickle we are. They just have that small piece of land on the edge of town, but Norrington has been threatening her as well."

Poor Charlotte was Jonas's older sister. She lived with their mother, whose life was a constant uphill battle. Mr. Blake had been a horrid piece of work, who abandoned the rest of the Blakes when Jonas was young. As Jonas grew into a kind, intelligent, capable young man, he was the apple of his mother's eye. Mrs. Blake was devastated when Jonas went away.

I could understand that.

"The thing is," Tom continued, "Charlotte's just had a letter from Jonas, and..."

My ears blocked Tom out at the mention of the letter. *Lucky Charlotte! To have news of him so often! To have a real relationship with him not bogged down with disappointed expectations! To think that I—*

"Annie..." Tom said softly, pulling on my bonnet strings. His eyes were kind, his face knowing.

I nodded.

"I was saying," he resumed, "that Jonas has distinguished himself in the militia. He's under a fellow named Nelson, who leads a bunch of troops about the southern colonies. They've just had some action in North Carolina, and Jonas says they're stopping there for the summer. They need the rest, he says, and this Nelson wants his men ready for more fighting when the time comes."

Jonas. Fighting. In the war.

"Annie?"

I looked up at Tom sharply. My eyes must have been wild with fear and emotion, for he put his good arm around me in a tight hug.

"He's fine, Annie. He's a sharp one. No redcoat is going to get the drop on Jonas Blake."

I nodded again quickly, my tongue unable to form words of agreement.

"My point is," Tom began again, speaking quickly lest my mind derail for a third time, "Jonas is close—just south of here into North Carolina. If we rode down there, we could ask him to come home and help us. Shoot, I bet he could bring some friends with him and really scare Norrington into leaving us alone."

I was all ears and attention now. "What? Bring Jonas here? Have you gone mad, Tom? Why would he come to help us after the way we treated him? How Father and Mother..." my words trailed away, lost in memory. I could not ride into the Carolinas and fetch Jonas. I could not. There had to be another way.

"Annie," Tom repeated, squeezing my shoulder. "His own mother and sister are in trouble too. It's not for the Summertons. It's for the whole town. And Jonas, prideful goose that he is, is a man of honor. If he's able, he will come, no matter what he thinks about you."

My, but those last words stung! The idea that Jonas even had thoughts about me, much less that they could be cast aside, caused a deep pain to flare inside. But Tom was right. Charlotte and Mrs. Blake were involved in this mess as well, and Jonas was indeed a man of honor. It was truly a remarkable endeavor and might possibly be successful.

"Let's do it." I sighed in defeat. "On one condition."

Tom grinned in relief. "Shoot."

My smile was small—just the barest of beginnings—but it helped. Hope began to simmer inside of me.

"You have to break it to Betsy."

Ah, Betsy. Being of nervous temperament, there was no way she would consent to stay behind with Father—knowing nothing, hearing no news until we returned. The poor girl would wring her hands plain off! No, she would need to join us. She was a hardy worker and an excellent cook, besides providing a calm and practical influence on Tom's and my otherwise lofty schemes.

And so, the three Summerton children would ride south to North Carolina, seeking help from a most unusual source.

We told no one of our errand.

It was probably wise for us to leave town as soon as possible, particularly with my recent foray into criminal activity. Or near it, anyway. Was it a crime to *want* to kill a man? To consider it for the barest of moments? I intended to not find out. Tom and I packed quickly—two changes of clothes apiece and all the food we could spare. Mary Hudgins—Tom's and my particular friend—agreed to stay at our house with Father while we were gone. She was fully aware of our precarious situation and would do her best to stave off questions as to our whereabouts.

It pained me deeply to leave town without speaking to Nate's parents, to help them grieve the loss of their son, to not even attend the funeral. But we had no time to spare, and it was a long ride down to North Carolina where the Virginia militia had just defeated the Cherokee.

Within a day we were on our way. We started on the straight path south with no idea what would befall us when we arrived.

IN WHICH I MAKE
A GRAVE MISTAKE

SUMMERTON FARM,
SEPTEMBER 1775

Only the promise of a new contraband novel from Mary Hudgins could minimize the uncomfortable effects of hay stabbing me along the spine. True, there were more appropriate places to read, but they generally involved my mother. And as she so disapproved of the activity—unless it was a stiff sermon or boring history—some ingenuity was required on my part. How quick witted was I to grasp my novel and hide it under my apron when Mother directed me to the barn to brush the horses. And now, that rapid and banal activity complete, I had time to lie in the loft and read until I was missed.

Fall was here, to be sure. The wind had changed in Virginia and in the colonies as well. News had trickled south that the British were marching on Philadelphia! Tongues were clicking; hands were wringing throughout our village. Which city would be next? True, we all trusted in our fair leader (and fellow Virginian) General Washington, who was planning to protect the City of Brotherly Love and restore it to our bosom, but the fervor of the war was slowly settling in.

One of our hands had left midsummer, with another planning to depart after the harvest was ended. The story was the same in various farms and homesteads across Sussex County. The exodus bothered me very little, being barely sixteen with more idle pursuits to apply myself to. These activities, coupled with my secret about Jonas, kept me plenty occupied.

Jonas himself appeared as I was beginning the fifth chapter of Mary's book.

"Psst! Anne!"

I glanced up from the small novel and grinned in delight. His sandy head was poking above the ladder, his arms resting in the loft at my feet. "What are you doing, goose?" he asked, giving my ankles a solid yank.

The movement upset my repose, stuffing an excess of hay into my petticoats and causing me to lose my place.

"Jonas! Ouch! Do not roughen me so! Now there is hay in my skirts."

Jonas laughed and launched himself into the loft beside me, merrily plucking hay from my slippers and their environs. The absurdity of the situation elicited a round of giggles from us both as we enjoyed a rare moment alone.

"Why are you not with Father?" I asked when the itching about my feet began to subside.

"He sent me to find some tools. And as I was searching for them, I found that somebody had brushed the horses and hastily left the brushes on the barn floor. Now who would drop their brushes in a fired-up hurry rather than replace them, except one who was burning to read a new novel? I ask you, Anne? Who? Hmm?"

I slid the novel under my hip. Jonas shared some of my mother's disapproval for idle reading. "I know nothing of what you speak, Jonas," I said, drawing another round of laughter.

He began to move toward the ladder.

"Where are you going? Are you already leaving?"

Jonas nodded. "I have duties to your father, my love. But I will see you this afternoon in the north pasture, as we'd planned. Bring none of that fluff you've buried in your skirts, do you hear?"

I surveyed my knees and nodded. "I'll leave the novel behind this time."

He grinned broadly, leaning forward to plant a kiss on my forehead. "Two o'clock," he reminded me.

I nodded. Two o'clock. Only a few hours.

Little did I know that two o'clock would dawn with more problems than Jonas and I could manage.

During the next several hours, the temperature dropped as a cold front rolled through our county. The trees shook violently in the wind as the air turned icy. I had planned to duck into the north pasture to meet Jonas after hanging Mother's linens on the line, as the view of the clothesline was obstructed from the kitchen window. However, the growing chill was too much to bear, so I dashed inside the house to fetch a shawl before making my way to Jonas.

Betsy, I learned later, happened to see me leave, and when my mother came searching for me, told her in which direction I had walked.

And so our secret was unceremoniously discovered that day when my parents found us, sitting shoulder to shoulder against a broad oak tree. Our hands were clasped, and Jonas's Bible was spread across our laps. That my parents would discover us in the most innocent of activities didn't signify in the least.

We did not hear my parents approaching us on the soft grass, weary from searching for me in the house, and so we were quite surprised when my mother's screech pierced the tranquility.

"Anne Summerton! Just *what* are you doing?"

We leaped to our feet. I immediately began to tremble with a vicious onset of nerves, but Jonas visibly calmed before my mother's rage.

"Isn't it obvious, dear?" my father interrupted. "It's plain that Anne and Jonas have formed an attachment."

"An attachment!" My mother's voice reached an even higher pitch. "That is impossible! Unbelievable! I'll not have it, Anne, I tell you I won't! He's a farmhand—not fit to marry either one of you! And Jonas Blake, what do you think you're—"

"That's enough for now, Elizabeth," my father ordered. He did not bellow or raise his voice as my mother had, but his gray eyes were grave as they rested on me for what seemed an interminable time.

"Father," I began, "I promise, Jonas and I were doing nothing dishonorable." I gestured toward the Bible, which Jonas had retrieved from the ground. "We were honestly just reading Scripture."

My father's eyes flickered to the Bible and back to my face. "Are you telling me you and Jonas do not have a romantic understanding?"

I had no confidence that our passion could save the day—no desire to thwart my parents and court the consequences: my mother's livid screams, my father's cold fury, or worse, forcing Jonas to go away. A stingy cowardice sheathed my heart as I saw a chance to salvage our secret. I looked faith and honesty in the face and turned my back on them.

"N—" I opened my mouth to send the lie flying, but it was blocked from its landing by Jonas.

"Yes, Mr. Summerton, we do have an understanding," he said solemnly, not looking in my direction.

My parents' faces were etched in shock and disapproval. Mother was red, trembling so violently with anger that I was sure she would burst through her skin.

Father's anger was the exact opposite. It was calm, but no less deadly. He gazed long at Jonas and me in turn, but when he finally spoke, all he said was, "We will discuss this in the house. Come."

He turned on his heel and began the long trek across the fields to the house, my mother following him stiffly. Jonas and I wordlessly joined them. When I found the courage, I cast a glance in his direction. I was keen to see if he had detected my floundering loss of valor, when I nearly lied about our love to save my own skin.

When his eyes met mine, they were at once chill with anger and rife with sadness. He had seen, and he had saved me from my own weakness.

"No. No. Absolutely not. Anne is not to marry one of our farmhands. He is completely unsuitable, Richard. For goodness' sakes, he lives in our *barn!*" My mother shook her head vehemently.

We were seated around our kitchen table—Mother, Father, Jonas, and me. Betsy and Tom were banished from the conversation, although I was sure they were lurking about close enough to listen.

"Allow him to speak, Elizabeth," my father said, watching Jonas and me levelly.

I sat dejected, my shoulders slumped, my face tear-stained, looking every bit the child that I was. Jonas, in contrast, sat tall and proud—not intimidated by my parents, but buoyed by the faith that kept him strong. He felt his purpose was sure, encouraged in his suit by the LORD himself.

"Thank you, Mr. Summerton," Jonas began. "I realize that I am nothing now—a mere farmhand. But I believe if I was given time, I could return with status and wealth, proving that I am worthy of your daughter."

Mother fumed, but remained silent. She couldn't bear to be defied, any more than she could bear to let me marry someone not of her choosing.

My father weighed Jonas's words, nodding slightly. "Well, you know I think you're a fine lad, Jonas: smart, honorable, and a good worker. But Anne is young, and I would need to see that you could offer her a more suitable life."

"Honorable!" My mother spat, interrupting without ceremony. "Sneaking around behind our backs with a young girl, doing who-knows-what when he's supposed to be working. I fail to see how that is honorable!" Her eyes narrowed at Jonas.

I shrank farther into my hard, wooden chair, but Jonas somehow grew taller beneath her tirade.

"Mrs. Summerton, I realize that Anne's and my behavior does indeed look devious, but we realized early on that Anne is young and our attachment needed to remain—discreet—for a time. But Mrs. Summerton, I assure you we have done nothing dishonorable. I would not treat a young woman thus. Certainly not one I intend to marry."

"You will *not* marry her." My mother seethed, and I was frightened by her intensity.

"Elizabeth, enough," my father ordered. He directed his attention to me. "Anne, do you wish to marry Jonas?"

I looked at Jonas and seemed to pull strength from the confidence that flowed from his blue eyes. He didn't smile at me, didn't speak for me. He simply stared hard into my soul, as was his way.

I sighed and nodded. "I do, Father."

"I see." He paused. "I tend to agree with your mother that you're quite young and not always responsible. Do you think you are old enough to make such a commitment?"

I nodded again. "I agree too, Father. I think I'm a trifle young."

Jonas appeared to deflate slightly next to me. We'd agreed countless times together that I was too young, but to agree aloud with my parents disunited our cause. My accord with my father, taken with my shameful near-lie out in the pasture, was an obvious blow to Jonas's resolve.

In the space of a moment, staring at me mutely, he seemed to ask, *Are you quite certain?*

A quirked eyebrow, a slight incline of my head, and Jonas visibly relaxed at my assent.

His silent entreaty gave me an opportunity to leave the relationship unscathed. But I was young, and I did love him so, and for all of my idleness and silliness, I *was* certain.

"Very well." Father nodded, unaware of our silent exchange. "This is my decision. Jonas, for the time being your engagement to my daughter is terminated. However, in two years' time, when Anne is seventeen, I will allow you to ask for her hand once again. If in those intervening years you have acquired some property and status to your name, I would be happy to consent to your engagement. As I said, I think you're a fine lad, Jonas, and I know you will make an exceptional man. Don't tie yourself to a wife before you've had a chance to do so."

I knew that Father was right, that his proclamation was reasonable. However, in my youth and romantic sensibilities, I was prepared for love to conquer all.

Jonas sighed and sat back, nodding politely at my father. "Thank you, sir. I believe that is fair." He began to push himself back from his chair.

"Where are you going, Jonas? I don't wish ill feelings between us."

Jonas smiled broadly, his confidence restored. "No ill feelings here, Mr. Summerton. I just thought that, with your permission, I might set off directly. The harvest is near finished, and I'd like to make my way in the world as soon as possible so I may return for Anne."

My mother glowered but said nothing.

Like an emotional chameleon, my dejected state turned to glowing pride as I beamed up at Jonas.

"I see," Father answered, obviously displeased to lose yet another farmhand. "Well, that is understandable, certainly. What do you plan to do?"

Jonas squared his shoulders. "Join the militia."

My body reacted immediately, outside of my mind's consideration or consent. I bolted out of my chair, eyes wide, chest heaving, and, leaving daintiness aside, poked Jonas in the chest.

"The militia? No, Jonas. *No!*" My voice rose in pitch. "I won't have you going off to war, Jonas. Not to get killed. Not on my account."

"Anne," my father interjected, "Jonas's suggestion is sound. The militia is an excellent place for a young man of honor and ability to distinguish himself. During wartime, there are fewer opportunities for him here. Jonas can quite literally insert himself into society if he has some distinctive military experience. That is the excellence of our colonies—we are not saddled by British class restrictions."

"If he *lives* he can insert himself into society. If he doesn't get shot by a British rifle first." I stormed out the door and let it slam behind me with a satisfying *smack*. However, my abrupt exit, while dramatic, left me no place to wander—particularly with the oncoming storm. In the end I found myself pacing the porch, beating my hand upon the rail.

Was I being unreasonable? I thought not. It was all too common in our village to hear of colonists losing their lives to British muskets. We were hearing varied reports of this *war*—it would be over by Christmas; it would never be over; Britain was about to relent; Britain would never relent. America felt strongly about gaining independence from its master, and so it seemed the fight would go on until the wounded master released its claim upon us. And though it sounded fearful and faithless, I didn't want Jonas to be a part of that.

Too soon I heard the door slam behind me, and I knew it was Jonas. I didn't turn to face him, but quickly felt his hands on my shoulders turning me toward him. He held my hands in his and gazed at me imploringly.

"Anne, you must let me do this."

I started shaking my head, but he continued.

"Anne, please let me endeavor to deserve you."

"Jonas!" I jerked my hands from his and placed them on my hips. "You *do* deserve me. It's madness to attempt to earn something you already have!"

With my impetuous words, my anger swelled—at Father, for his frustrating demands, and at Jonas, for his steadfast willingness to obey them. I continued my invective, speaking as brashly as possible, unhindered by the path of destruction they might leave behind.

"What do you know about being a soldier? You're a farmer, not a minuteman. You will surely get yourself killed."

Jonas bore my argument stoically, but I could see that I was striking a raw nerve. I recalled our conversation of the previous winter, when he told me about the emotional wound left by his wayward father. He was emotionally cold, never showing Jonas or his sister any affection. For years the Blake family lived in tense silence, until one day Samuel Blake announced he was leaving. When Jonas—a young lad of ten—offered to accompany his father to aid him in his travels, Samuel had responded with a gruff, "Help? How could you help? You're of no use to me, boy. Never have been any good to me. None of you are."

This irreparable damage occurred when Jonas was only a boy, but it left its mark on Jonas the man. His flawless work ethic and ironclad honesty were results of that wound; he was driven by an inner desire to be valuable, to prove his mettle to his absent father. My insinuations about his inadequacy in battle were just heaping salt into it.

Finding I had struck him, I gladly continued. "I would rather you go away forever, Jonas, and live, than to dash off and die on a fool's errand."

As soon as the words left my mouth I regretted them, for I could see that my words had struck deep. He stiffened and leaned away from me—the soft, hopeful look upon his face vanished.

"So for me to gain success in the army is a fool's errand, is it?" His demeanor was calm as he said this, but he was angrier than I'd seen him.

Looking at his face, I realized I'd rather see him angry than pursuing me to his death on the battlefield.

"Yes," I answered, summoning my mother's snobbery into my voice. "It is. You'll be fighting Britain's most accomplished regulars, men trained their entire lives to be soldiers. How can you compete against that? Farmhands against the British army?" I snorted. "I think not!"

I was bringing some post-office gossip into this; in truth I had no idea what the redcoats were like. But I would press my advantage when the opportunity arose, however fabricated was my evidence.

Jonas's face was all pride against my barbs. He leaned in close to my face, all trace of tenderness gone, replaced with almost palpable fury. "Well, Anne, I suppose I will learn the truth of that soon enough. Although I can see that you don't much care."

"Actually," I remarked disdainfully, "I don't. You're being a fool, and I don't care to marry a fool!"

I instantly wished I could recall my words—I would sooner have hot coal placed to my lips like Isaiah than to see Jonas hurt by my declaration. But if I recalled my words, he would surely go to the army to win me, and I mustn't let that happen.

Suddenly Jonas turned and stalked to the barn, his gait taut and angry. I leaned against the pillar and began to cry. Within moments, Tom joined me. He slid his good arm around my shoulders and sighed.

"Oh, Anne," he muttered.

"Can't you talk some sense into him, Tom?"

"Anne, listen," Tom turned me toward him and stared me down. "Jonas knows his own mind. He's a stout man, a good man, and you can't prevent him from learning the truth of that."

Of course Tom was right. Jonas *was* a good man, the best of men. And now that I had chased him away from the militia, he would live to make his mark on the world in whatever way he pleased.

"At least I convinced him not to join the militia," I said, looking away from Tom's penetrating gaze. "If he hates me, there's no reason for him to scamper off. He can hate me here, safe at the farm."

Tom shook his head reproachfully. "Is that what you're after? You're a fool, Annie, and what's more, you don't know Jonas Blake."

The door to the barn creaked and caught our attention. It was quickly evident that Tom was correct—Jonas was leaving, his tan wool coat buttoned to his collarbone and his gray knapsack slung over his shoulder.

I began to shake. "Oh, no. No."

Tom squeezed my shoulder. "Let him go, Annie. If he is successful, he'll return for you." I shook his arm free and ran across the porch, down the steps, and began to follow Jonas down the lane.

"Jonas!" I shouted. "Please wait!"

He slowed just barely, allowing me to catch up with him. I clutched his arm and turned him toward me, pained to see the anger and hurt plainly etched on his face.

"Why are you *doing* this?"

Jonas took a deep breath and spoke slowly, in a deceptively calm and steady manner. "Anne, I *need* to do this. It is an opportunity to take risks and act valiantly and mature into the man God desires me to be. Regardless of our attachment, your father is right—working as a farmhand doesn't afford such prospects."

"But you could die!" I wailed, stamping my foot in the dusty lane. "I won't have it, Jonas! I won't!"

Jonas brought a hand to my cheek and spoke softly. "It will be worth it. You must have faith that this time apart will strengthen us. In the end, we will be thankful."

I whispered my response, every word paining us both. "*No,* it wouldn't be worth it—not if it takes your life. I would prefer us to be alive and apart, than for you to be courageous and die in battle."

He dropped his hand, shaking his head in frustration. "You would choose to end our engagement? Is my growth as a man less important than your own complacency? Your contentment at the expense of my improvement? Anne, such selfishness is not a function of a mature relationship."

Drawing a deep breath, I quickly considered his accusation. I envisioned a day two years hence when Jonas would return, decorated with a commission in General Washington's army. Father would be proud. Mother would be pleased. Jonas and I would marry and move to Williamsburg and attend fashionable parties, traveling in the highest circles of society.

Or Jonas could join a skirmish with the Indians in a week's time and fall to a Cherokee arrow. The other half of myself—gone in an instant.

Perhaps Tom was wrong about Jonas. If I removed his reason to prove himself, perhaps he would stay.

"Very well," I declared, summoning my last reserve of strength to jut my chin out stubbornly. "I will end our engagement if you join the militia."

The muscles in Jonas's jaw clenched as he stared at a point behind my head; perhaps he too was staring at that desirable point in our Williamsburg future, watching it dissolve in bitterness. After an interminable moment, he looked at me, but he was already far away.

"Good-bye, Anne."

PART TWO:
THE JOURNEY

THE COMMONWEALTH OF
VIRGINIA AND THE COLONY OF
NORTH CAROLINA, JUNE 1777

IN WHICH WE TAKE
IN THE SCENERY

It took us ten long days to ride from our farm south into the Carolinas—fielding dusty roads, tenacious storms, and our own lack of direction. We Summertons managed, however, through shameless blame shifting and dogged cynicism.

DAY ONE:

"Are you two crazy? I really can't believe we're doing this. These roads could be crawling with redcoats—we could be captured and taken to a British prison! Anne, what would they do to us in a British prison? And how do you think Jonas can help? Wasn't he a *farmhand* the last time we saw him? What makes you think he can do anything for us? What a waste of time this is!"

"Then you should have stayed home with Father, Bets."

"Tom, somebody has to keep you and Anne straight. And I'm the one that's good with direction … Anne?"

"Yes, Betsy?"

"Didn't you and Jonas quarrel before he went away?"

"Yes, Betsy."

"Then why do you think he'll help us?"

I shifted my gaze to Tom, rolling my eyes and pulling a face as when we were children. He leaned close to speak in my ear.

"You wanted to bring her."

"Neither of us knows how to cook, Tom."

He shrugged. "So? I could deal with tinned soup for a week if it meant peace and quiet."

Betsy, seeing our bent heads, hollered from behind. "What are you two whispering about? Don't leave me out of the conversation!"

DAY TWO:

"I think we've been riding west instead of south."

DAY THREE:

Persistent rain was an unpleasant addition to our journey.

"Tom?"

"Hmm?"

"Are you awake?"

"Somewhat."

"Do you mind listening to me for a few moments?"

"Well, Anne, seeing as it's raining and the three of us are crammed underneath this rhododendron bush, my options for amusements are threefold—sleep, listen to Betsy rant, check the horses. Sleep, answer Betsy's many questions, check the horses. Then sleep again. So no, Anne, I don't mind hearing what you have to say."

I hesitated.

"But see here, Anne, tantamount to the act of listening is you actually speaking. Conversation is funny that way."

"Do you think we're doing the right thing?"

"I think it's possible that Jonas can help us."

"Hmm. The response, 'Yes, Annie, I do think we're doing the right thing,' is curiously missing from that statement, Thomas."

Thomas sighed. "Annie, this is a difficult situation. Possibly the hardest that we will ever have to face—Father dying any day now; Norrington angling to take our farm, even harm us; Nate being murdered. That's not even mentioning the war. People do crazy things in times such as these. Our home and family are being threatened—I can't think of any better reason to go on an uncertain mission to see someone from our past that may or may not be able to help us."

I hesitated once more.

"Do you think he'll help?"

"If he's able, yes, I think he will."

"Despite me?"

Thomas chuckled. "Conceited, ain't you? What makes you think you'll have anything to do with it?"

"You're right. He's probably over the whole thing by now."

"Annie, it's been nearly two years gone since you and Jonas quarreled. We haven't had a letter from him, although he's certainly written to his mother and sister. And he's not had a normal life since then. It's not as if he's been tending his farm, learning a trade, or traveling with the preacher. He's been fighting for his life, Anne. Every day, maybe. The rules of forgiving and forgetting are different when a man's living that type of life."

I sighed. "How are you so wise, Thomas?"

Thomas chuckled. "Lot of good it's done me. Living with my two sisters—one crazy and one angry all the time. I'm the only sane person on the farm, except for Father, and he's so ill you can't tell."

DAY FOUR:

"Okay, I think we're going south now."

DAY FIVE:

I fervently prayed as we draw ever closer.

"God, I'm going to stick my neck out here and send some prayers up heaven's way. I know that I have been...well...rather spiteful and petty since Jonas left and Mother and Father took ill. But, really, what did you expect, God? First Jonas leaves. Then Mother dies...so suddenly...before I really forgave her for Jonas...and then Father so close to death, right after Mother. And me, who was never good at anything but being idle, in charge of Summerton. Surely you can't expect a girl to be cheerful through all of that, God, can you? Isn't that a bit much?"

There was no answer from God, although he was surely listening.

DAY SIX:

"Okay, Betsy, I think we've made it into North Carolina now. You can stop worrying about us getting lost. Again."

"What do you intend to do now, Thomas, start stopping at every farmhouse and asking where Nelson's militia is camped?"

"I just might, Bets. I just might."

Betsy snorted from the rear.

Day Seven:

I was not feeling well. The combination of hard riding, ill sleep, and very little food had its effect on my body. Luckily, Tom and Betsy seemed to be holding up well. Perhaps the farm work had rendered my body weaker than theirs. I hoped not.

Day Eight:

"He would have done what I asked, you know, Tom."

"What?"

"Jonas. When I asked him to stay, he would have."

"You've got your history wrong, Annie. You did ask. He said no."

My pride was singed beyond recognition. I had nothing to say to that.

After a moment, Tom continued, "Mother wouldn't let you marry him anyway."

"Nor Father."

"I think Father would have relented eventually. He was right fond of Jonas, you know. But Mother..."

I sighed. "She had an iron-clad will, didn't she? I couldn't ever get along with her."

Thomas snorted. "Maybe that's because when two mules get together for a parlay, all they can ever do is butt their hard heads together."

"Oh, that ain't even so! I am not stubborn like Mother."

"You keep telling yourself that, Annie."

"What are you two talking about?"

"Nothing, Betsy."

"Hey, Bets?"

"What is it, Anne?"

"Do you think I'm stubborn and hard like Mother?"

"I think you have all the best parts of her, Anne."

I was stunned into grateful silence.

"Except her beautiful eyes ... which you have, Bets."

"Thanks, Anne."

DAY NINE:

I attempted to pray again.

"LORD, I realize that last time I tried to pray I got off-track about my own conceits, and I apologize. You can see I'm rusty. I have turned my back on you these many months, and I am sorry. I feel you calling to me, and I am trying to listen. I know that you are the only one who can truly help us, and I guess I pray you make Jonas willing. I don't know what kind of craziness you put into Tom to give him this idea, but I sure hope it works.

"Please, God, help me to follow you and not to trot down a path of my own. That has gone ill for me in the past. Help me to trust you fully, because I'm still sore from these two years of hurt.

"Will Jonas help, God? Will he? Does he hate me still? Worse, does he love me still? That would also be difficult, as I am nowhere near the soft, sweet Anne he once knew. Either option is frightening, LORD. I can't consider either without trembles alighting on my body.

"I haven't been truly faithful in years, LORD, but I aim to try, since this world is too big for me to handle on my own.

"I guess that's an Amen."

DAY TEN:

As I felt like we were finally drawing close, my body rebelled. I was tired and weak as I sat in the saddle. A soft bed would have remedied this, but I did not envision one in my future.

DAY ELEVEN:

"Pardon me, sir?"

"Can I help you, son?"

"Yessir. My sisters and I are looking for General Nelson's Virginia Militia. We hear they've stopped in these parts for the month."

"Oh, yes, indeed. They are camped about eight miles south of here, down by the Chowan River. See that creek there?"

"Yessir."

"Follow it south, and turn west when you reach the river. You'll find them all there."

"I'm obliged, sir."

"You're welcome, son … Do you know somebody in that regiment?"

"Yes, sir … a friend of the family."

"I see. You might want to keep an eye on your sisters around some of those boys … if you catch my meaning?"

Betsy screeched. "What meaning?"

"Hush, Betsy!"

"But, Anne, what does he—"

Tom hastily interrupted, "Yes, sir. I certainly will. Thank you for the advice."

There were eight miles. Only eight miles.

IN WHICH WE FORM SOME
NEW ACQUAINTANCES

"Psst, Anne," Tom whispered from his scouting place. "I found it."

I looked up from my rough survey of the ground. Never one for tracking, most of my efforts paled in comparison to Tom's. Four hours had passed since our encounter with a local farmer—four hours spent roaming empty woods looking for a mythical camp. The sight of the dusty track was a welcome relief—Betsy and I could stop pretending that we were tracking and do something useful.

After obtaining our mounts, we wordlessly began our trot toward the camp. I couldn't help but wonder for the dozenth time if this was a fool's errand. If we were successful in finding help, would that assistance be enough to fight off the growing tide of corruption in our beloved village? And would Father's health last long enough to keep his tenuous grasp on our farm during our absence?

It was near dark when we heard men's laughter, smelled the embers of a fire, and saw its light shining through the trees. Immediately dismounting, we tied the horses and crept closer to the sound. We paused at the edge of the tree line and squatted on our heels, mutually aware that barging into the camp was unadvisable.

"Well," I whispered, "what do we do now? Who's going in there?"

The silence of my siblings was deafening and told me clearly their opinion on the matter. I held my tongue and allowed it to drag on interminably, not letting Tom and Betsy stay quiet, but forcing them to speak the uncomfortable truth.

"Anne," Betsy finally said, "I think you need to go."

"She's right, Anne. It's not the most courageous thing for me to send my sister into a camp of crazed soldiers. But this is our last hope, Anne. You know it is. It must be you."

"Why me? I'm the one who sent him away angry, remember?"

Tom's eyes bored into mine. "Anne, you know Betsy can't go." He gazed toward our anxiety-ridden sister. "She would lose her composure in an instant."

"Why not you, Tom?"

He barked out a sarcastic laugh. "Hugging my arm and dragging my foot behind me? Hardly a display of power, Anne, wouldn't you say?"

There was no time to be emotional. My feminine wiles were left on the farm. Even so, as I stood I brushed off my skirts and kicked the mud off my boots. My glance at Betsy was a silent appeal. She wiped the dirt from my cheeks and re-rolled my hair, then nodded silently. Tom squeezed my arm, and I stepped forward into the clearing, making my way slowly toward the circle of tents.

The voices grew louder as I reached the outskirts of the camp, which was nothing more than a score of tents and a smattering of fires. The closest tent stood open, its flaps propped wide, a fierce poker game underway. I took a deep breath and waited to be seen. A step farther was all that was required, and a young soldier my age looked up from his cards. His dark brown eyes quickly registered the shock of seeing me there, and then his face gave way to an unattractive leer. Glancing around the table, he garnered the attention of his counterparts.

"Looky what's walked on into our tent, boys," he said, eyeing me up and down.

I wasn't prepared for this particular reaction. Quickly, I began to shuffle backward, out of the tent and toward the center of the camp.

"Um, excuse me, gentlemen," I stuttered, inwardly fuming at the misuse of the word on such a slovenly band of miscreants. "I seem to have stumbled into the wrong tent."

The leering young soldier pushed his chair back and staggered away from his table. His companions followed suit.

"Not so fast, missy," he said, and a murmur of agreement rose up from the group. "Why don't you join our game?"

"Oh, I don't think so, boys," my voice rose as I spoke. Hopefully it would alert other, less interested soldiers.

My wish was granted; a tent flap to my left whooshed open, and another young soldier glared in my direction.

"Hey, what's all the … man-alive, it's a *girl!*" He was as friendly as the others, unfortunately.

A group of soldiers followed him out of the tent, and suddenly I found myself surrounded by eager, ogling young men, a dozen in number—all closing in slowly on my shaking and shuddering form. I momentarily closed my eyes, praying, hoping for anything that would help me out of this mess. The group of men began to argue over who saw me first. Their voices were a bleating, angry din that rose in my ears, just barely audible over the heartbeat pounding in my ears. I opened my eyes; the poker player—obviously the boldest of the group—was lifting his hand to touch my hair, when a booming roar echoed from behind me.

"What the on earth is going on here?"

The young soldiers scattered quickly, all except the card player, who was rooted in his spot by the clear dominance of the newcomer behind us.

"Hanson? Do you have an explanation for why you are out of your tent with your mates, here?"

"Sir, yes. We were, um, well, distracted by this … "

"This young lady?"

I was frozen, caught in the middle of this exchange. The new soldier, who obviously carried some authority, was behind me. My back remained turned on my rescuer; I would keep my tongue until I could explain my reason for being in this clearly inappropriate place.

"Yes, sir," Hanson said, his voice shaking now. "She stumbled into our tent, and ... "

"And asked to be hounded and molested by you animals?" the man interrupted, his voice now dangerously calm.

"No! No, sir."

"Did you, miss?" the officer addressed my back directly.

I shook my head but didn't speak. A gentle hand was laid on my elbow and slight pressure applied in his direction.

"Hanson, you're dismissed ... You know, miss"—his voice lowered to a more congenial, yet still quite stern tone, as he pulled me around to face him— "a militia camp is not the place for a ... "

The gentle voice came to a rushing halt as our faces met. My body was flooded with two conflicting emotions—a pulsing pain shooting through my hardened heart, and relief that my mission was at an end.

" ... lady," finished Jonas hotly, his ice-blue eyes narrowed into a contemptuous glare.

IN WHICH I TAKE ILL

Jonas's hand clamped my elbow tightly as he pulled me swiftly across the remainder of the camp. A larger tent, obviously in better care than the others, was erected a few yards away from the rest. A crackling fire burned before it, bathing it in warm light that was uncomfortable in the balmy summer evening. Jonas lifted one of the flaps and shoved me roughly inside.

The living quarters were neatly kept, clean as could be. A small cot was tucked into the corner, a square table fitted snugly at its side; I spied his Bible perched atop its smooth surface. A large desk sat at the opposite corner, strewn with maps and various papers, a canteen, and silver-rimmed eyeglasses. An open trunk sat against one wall, clothes neatly folded inside, and a dark uniform coat hung from a cord tied at the tent's corners. It was these personal items—his clothes especially, and his Bible—that gave my heart its final squeeze, and the intensity of the last few minutes descended upon me. My breath began to heave in ragged gasps. I clutched my stomach and tried to steady myself.

Jonas, who had been standing immobile at the entrance to the tent, finally thawed and began to move. His long legs propelled him across the tent in two strides. He grasped my shoulders as I began to keel. "Anne, are you all right? Anne?"

I wasn't. The wear of the last week's ride had finally reached its limit. My body was hot and cold, rigid yet fluid—a confused muddle of sensations. I shook his hands from me, wagging my head and fumbling my way to his cot.

"I just need to lie down a minute, Jonas," I mumbled, reveling in the sensation of the cot and the soft pillow—not my bed at Summerton yet far better than the ground. The last thing I recall before passing into a much-needed rest was begging Jonas to find my siblings.

I awoke to the sound of Betsy's voice.

"I'm so glad we found you, Jonas."

"Well, Anne is lucky I showed up when I did. It was madness for you two to allow her to come here alone. Those young fools could have hurt her, could have—" He stopped abruptly.

His accusation resonated in the moment of silence that followed.

"I know," Tom said. "We just thought she'd be the best to . . ." his words trailed away lamely.

I opened my eyes. My aching head was fuzzy. I could see Jonas's small table in front of me—his mother's Bible lay in my peripheral vision. A dark blue wool blanket was pulled up to my chin; it smelled strongly of clean soap and of Jonas. The potency of this attack on my senses nearly rendered me faint, but before dizziness could claim me, Jonas noticed that I was stirring. His tall frame passed my line of vision as he knelt beside me.

"You're awake."

Finally I was able to look at him, to take in the sight of his features and discern how the years had treated him. The blue eyes were still clear and hard, his skin drawn taut over his cheekbones, tan and weathered from time spent outdoors. His light brown hair had grown long; it curled over his shoulder blades in a loose queue. Although the hard times showed plainly, his spirit and pride were still very much apparent. Yes, he was the same Jonas, and that was a relief.

A weary smile crossed his face. "I believe the sight of my kingly accommodations rendered you faint, Miss Anne," he said.

My voice faltered. I returned his weary smile.

Betsy spoke up. "When we heard the commotion, Tom followed you into the camp and caught sight of you two coming in here. He doubled back to fetch me, and we just missed your fainting spell. When we arrived you were lying in the bed, which was a surprise! It gave me quite a fright."

Did I detect a light of whimsy in her eyes? *Whimsy?* At such a time as this? She was ridiculous.

I managed to find my voice. "I did *not* faint." I struggled to sit up.

Jonas stood up and backed away from the cot, while Betsy rushed to take his place. I leaned against his pillow, willing my body to strengthen, but feeling no relief.

"Tom, did you tell Jonas why we've come?"

Jonas cleared his throat. "Yes, he told me about the whole unfortunate mess."

"It's been really terrible these last months," I said, surprised at the hoarseness of my voice. "Will Norrington has become a bit of a terror in town."

"Yes, Jonas," Betsy continued. "He killed Nate Wilkins, and nobody did a thing about it."

"Nate Wilkins? From that family up in Carlton?" Jonas asked.

Memories of a laugh-filled dance at our barn raising filled my head.

No, no, no, I thought. *Betsy, please hold your tongue, you wretched girl! Don't tell him—*

"Yes, indeed, that's him! He *was* Anne's betrothed," Betsy declared.

It seemed her words were louder and coarser for the effect they had. As for me, who should have delicately dropped my eyes to allow Jonas his moment of shock, I couldn't turn away. It was like that day in the street was Nate was killed—the sensible thing to do was to run for help, but I was drawn to disaster. And so I was with Jonas. I couldn't bear to avert my gaze, but insisted on watching the effect this news had on him.

Oh, but I regretted my eager scrutiny! Jonas's blue eyes seemed to freeze, and his face noticeably hardened. It was as if every defense that could be mustered was thrown into his countenance, arming it as a battlement. His lips were a grim line, his brow a deep furrow. The only indication of sentiment was a slight crinkle at the corner of his cold eyes.

He refused to look at me for a lengthy moment; in that time I watched him regain control over his emotion. When at last his anger calmed, his frosty glare swung to me.

"Betrothed?" His voice was wintry enough to make me shiver under his stiff blanket.

Then, finally, I had the grace to drop my eyes. "Times are hard all around, Jonas," I said softly, my gaze cast toward the floor. "Sometimes, young women must marry to have a provider. And with Father so ill—"

"We didn't know who else to turn to, Jonas," Tom said, saving me. He was seated across the tent at Jonas's desk. "We'd heard of your success in the militia, and I asked your sister if she knew where we could find you."

I heard the disbelief in Jonas's voice. "You three rode all the way here from Abbingdon?"

Tom nodded. "Yep. Took us ten days."

Jonas eyed Tom's stiff, mostly useless leg with sympathy. "*Ten?* What did you do, ride up to Williamsburg and then cut south?"

Tom glared at Betsy and me in turn. Jonas glanced at the three of us, then passed his hand over his brow and sighed.

"Could you use some ale, Thomas?"

Tom grinned. "I could, Jonas."

Jonas nodded. "All right, then. Come with me. Ladies, you should by all accounts *not* be here, so I'll thank you to stay put." He nodded stiffly in our direction and showed Tom out of the tent.

Betsy and I were left alone.

"Well," Betsy said, "don't he beat all. *Captain* Blake."

"Captain?" I whispered, beginning to feel sick. The tent seemed to close in on me, and I felt my body lean to the side. With Jonas and Tom gone, I felt it most prudent to rest. Perhaps Jonas's mood would improve during the night.

"Bets, I am going back to sleep. Wake me if the British show up."

"And what am I to do with the men gone and you slumbering away?"

I had no strength to answer her, only drifted once more into a foggy sleep.

When I awoke it was dark in the tent, save for a lantern sitting on Jonas's makeshift desk. He and Betsy and Tom were huddled around it, murmuring in hushed tones.

"Betsy," I whispered, my mouth parched.

"She's awake." My sister, an excellent nurse from her experience with my father, leapt up from her chair and came to the cot. She touched my head.

"Anne, you're burning up with fever. Jonas…"

Jonas was immediately by my side. My senses were so dulled, I couldn't imagine how quickly he'd arrived there. His brow furrowed as he placed his cool hand on my cheeks and forehead.

"Jonas," I murmured, reaching for his hand. He quickly snatched it away.

"She *is* quite warm," he agreed. "I'll go and speak to the medic. Why don't you two bunk down and get some rest?"

I found rest difficult, even in my illness. At length Jonas returned and sat outside the tent with Tom, thinking me asleep. Instead I lay on my back, staring at the top of the tent, craving a breeze in the small, stuffy space. Betsy was beside me, already asleep. I could just discern the glow of the fire outside the tent where Jonas and Tom sat talking.

"So he really said that, then?" Jonas's voice was quiet and decidedly *not* calm.

"That's what we hear," Tom answered. "You can't really blame Nate for being angry."

"I would have gutted that disgusting fool, and Anne's not even my *betrothed*." He spit the last word out as if it was an ill taste in his mouth.

Tom wisely sat quiet for a moment.

"Why did she come here?" Jonas asked. I could barely hear him, but could well detect the frustration in his voice.

"It's our home, Jonas," Tom said. "And you must understand how difficult it actually was for Anne to make this journey. We wouldn't have considered it had we not seen your sister the day Nate was killed."

Jonas didn't answer immediately. The silence seemed to drag on forever as I awaited his answer, barely breathing. My stays were suddenly too tight, the air in the tent even closer and stuffier than ten seconds previous.

When Jonas finally spoke, his voice was tired and warm with feeling. "Your sister wrenched me in two, Tom. A man's not easily over that. I don't know that I can forgive her, but my heart is such in the habit of loving her..."

"I know it's difficult, Jonas."

Quiet stretched for a few long moments.

When Jonas next spoke, his voice was steely and hard. "I cannot love her again," he said with finality, "but I cannot watch her suffer, either. I will come to help in appreciation of what she used to mean to me."

His words pained me. I expected nothing else, deserved nothing more, but I felt despair set in again nonetheless. Jonas had been buried away for these two years past; to have him resurrected here in my presence, only to hear his cold dismissal of me, was difficult to bear.

The conversation lapsed for several minutes. I heard nothing but Betsy's breathing and the crackle of the fire outside. Sleep had almost claimed me when Jonas spoke again.

"Did she love him?"

Neither Tom nor I needed to wonder of whom Jonas spoke. Tom took several moments to frame his response, and I listened closely. Recognizing that we were two sides of the same coin, I was intrigued to hear his reply.

"You have to comprehend what Annie's life has been like the past year, Jonas," he began. "She was devastated after you left, and she was angry with Mother and Father for how they handled your attachment." He paused, trying to adequately depict my state of mind so Jonas would understand. "Then Mother died, and while Father's physical health was fine for a while, his mind and his heart retreated. With me unable to do much work, and Betsy as nervous as she is, everything fell on Anne's shoulders. When Father turned sick, Anne's burden grew even heavier, and this with most of the younger men and farmhands leaving town to fight. By the time Father took to his bed, there were few men for ten miles around under the age of forty. Anne was the head of household, head of the farm … it's quite a load for a girl that previously loved nothing more than reading stolen novels."

Jonas laughed softly at the memory of my lost youth. "Yes, she did like to do that."

"Nate was a quiet man, but a good man. He treated her well—he would have made her a good husband. I reckon that Anne thought of saving the farm when she accepted him. It was clear that when she was with Nate, she didn't have to be the caretaker anymore. He took care of her, and she needed that. I … we … *needed* to see her taken care of."

"Well, I am glad that is so," Jonas said. "But it irks me all the same."

"Now, I never did see her laugh or smile like she did when she was with you," Tom offered.

Jonas said nothing.

"But then again, Anne has done little enough of that the past two years, anyway."

There was another long pause, and then talk turned to the war, to crops, to Jonas's mother and sister. I faded into sleep, burning with fever and melancholy.

That night, in my fever-ridden dreams, an angel came to visit me. His touch was cool and soft. He bathed my head and my arms with something that made my skin tingle; it soothed my hot and flushed body.

He hummed while he worked, a tune familiar to me yet nothing I would ever recall. As he smoothed the hair from my forehead, he prayed for me.

"LORD, lift her up on wings like eagles. Protect her. Heal her sick body. Send your angels concerning her. Keep her safe from the enemy. She is yours. Please keep her wrapped in your protective arms."

I felt light and airy after his prayer; the oppressive heat of my fever seemed to lessen while he was there.

I liked that angel. He was much more pleasant than Jonas.

"Anne," a gruff whisper awoke me from my dream.

"Angel?" I mumbled. "Please help me feel better, angel."

"Oh, Anne, come now. Wake up." A hand shook my shoulder roughly.

I opened my eyes to Jonas, his face several inches away. He must have been kneeling down next to the cot. I felt Betsy's form asleep next to me; the heat of her body was overbearing.

"I'm hot," I said.

"Yes, you are. You have a fever. Here, you need to sit up and drink this." He held a cup out in front of my face.

I was so weak I merely stared up at him, completely incapable of moving toward the drink.

Jonas seemed to sense my difficulty and was clearly exasperated. He sighed and leaned down toward me, sliding his arm behind my shoulders to lift them up. His touch was like a thousand tiny tingles across my back. I shivered.

"I'm sorry." He attempted to push my torso upright.

I was honestly trying to hold myself erect, but was thoroughly exhausted. I recalled how poorly I'd felt the last three days of our trip. Perhaps I was truly ill and hadn't realized it.

"I'm sorry, Jonas," I said. Frustrated tears began falling down my cheeks. "I can't."

He heaved another great sigh. "All right, Anne—come, now."

He lifted my shoulders again and sat behind me, supporting me with his arm and torso. My back was against his broad chest, his leg bent and planted at my hip. This was the most Jonas and I had ever touched, even throughout the time of our attachment. Perhaps I was delirious, but this realization was in equal parts amusing and sad.

I giggled, which irritated him further.

"Can you please help me now?" he snapped.

His arm curled in front of me, holding the cup in front of my face. His other arm hung away from me stiffly. I managed to lift a hand and place it on his wrist, guiding the cup to my lips. The first sip stung my mouth, which was so dry and swollen it barely absorbed any of the liquid. I coughed from the effort and waited a few moments before trying again. I could feel the pounding of Jonas's heart behind mine and then wondered if it was my own. We sat in that manner—like lovers but far from it—for nearly a quarter hour as I sipped the medicine little by little until it was gone.

"That's all," I whispered hoarsely, dropping Jonas's wrist for the last time.

He gently extracted his frame from behind me and laid me back onto the cot. The effort had sapped what little strength I'd gained from my rest. My eyes fluttered as sleep threatened to claim me once more.

"Thank you, Jonas."

He nodded stiffly, but didn't say anything.

"I'm so sorry, Jonas ... so sorry," I mumbled as I drifted into sleep.

His eyes were troubled as he watched me go.

IN WHICH JONAS
MAKES A DECISION

When I awoke I could faintly detect dawn light shining between the tent flaps. Betsy still breathed evenly in the cot beside me. My fever had broken. I was still weak but not delirious, and no longer overcome with sickness. However, I had a scorching thirst. Lifting up on my elbow, I glanced at the table next to the cot and saw a mug of water. My thick, cottony tongue immediately began to swell, and I focused on my goal. Sweeping my eyes around, I glimpsed Jonas; he was asleep on the floor next to the cot. His face was serene, and I envied him. I imagined he was probably at peace until I appeared, and only in sleep was there respite from his complicated emotions. I reached down and softly brushed his brow with my fingers. His hand instantly shot up and grasped my wrist as his eyes flew open. They bore into me like blue beams, and I gasped in surprise.

"I'm sorry, I..."

"What ails you, Anne?" he whispered, letting go of my hand quickly. "Do you want for something?"

I cast my eyes down to the floor, embarrassed. "I am feeling better... but I am thirsty."

Jonas sat up, reaching behind him to retrieve the mug from the table. He handed it to me, and I drank. The water cooled and soothed me. I handed him the mug.

"Thank you." I lay back onto the cot.

We sat silently and watched the dim light grow stronger.

Jonas was part of Nelson's Lower Virginia militia, which had been traveling in the Carolinas for many months now. The militia throughout the colonies saw very little action in those early years; they were called on mainly to prevent slave uprisings and control the Tory population. If a soldier distinguished himself in the militia, he might be recruited to fight in the Continental Army with General Washington himself. According to the British, the militia of the American colonies was in general a disorganized band of rabble. They were poorly outfitted, poorly clothed, and not nearly as well organized as their enemies. But they were fighting to rid themselves of a cumbersome burden, and that gave them a fervor the redcoats lacked.

Jonas's regiment was camped by the river for the summer, awaiting the Frenchman Lafayette. It was hoped he would bring several thousand of his well-armed countrymen and turn the tide for the Patriots. Generals up and down the coast were readying their troops for a new offensive against the British, and Nelson's militia was among those looking forward to another push.

That morning, Tom, Betsy, and I stayed in Jonas's tent, while he conferred with Nelson. We spent this unexpected downtime differently—Tom paced, dragging his leg lightly along the tent floor; I slept, still trying to regain strength from my bout with the fever; and Betsy continued to rant and worry.

"What does he think he's going to do? Tear out of here and leave the army waiting for him?"

Tom glanced at me, confirming that he shared Betsy's concern. It was a valid fear, after all. Although the regiment was supposedly stationary for the summer, a summons could come any time for them to mobilize and march on their bedraggled feet to a new destination. And Jonas would go with them. For a moment I was as riddled with fear as my siblings. I considered Jonas's position in the army, his disdain for me, and the slim chance of his being able to help.

My God, I thought, *why on earth am I here?*

Panic settled in. I was momentarily frozen. My siblings needed me to be strong, but I had no hope to share with them. I opened my mouth to agree with them, to apologize for my inability to allay their fears, when a strange and soothing presence took root in my sternum and bubbled through my torso. This sensation washed my heart, and eventually my mind, with unbridled peace. It was altogether unaccountable, but I knew Jonas would help us. After all, his mother and sister shared our predicament. It had nothing whatsoever to do with me, and yet I was still sure.

"Tom, Betsy," I said with strange confidence, "Jonas will find a way. Or God will."

Betsy looked at me as if I was mad. Her violet eyes widened in surprise, then narrowed at me suspiciously. She sauntered toward me, her hands on her plump hips. "God?" she asked. "It's been a while since you've cared about God, Anne."

Betsy spoke the truth. It had been a while, but in the days since Nate's death, I'd been feeling a potent sense of purpose. Sometimes it mingled pleasantly with peace and sometimes not. However, the purpose was always accompanied by his presence, so I was assured it was not of my own making. It was with this peace that I climbed out of Jonas's cot, giving my face and neck a thorough washing, combing my hair, and sifting through our scanty reserve of clothing.

"That is true, Bets," I said. "But he is trustworthy, even if I am not."

"Anne," Tom asked, distracting me, "what are you doing?"

I turned toward him with a steel grey gaze, feeling my old strength rushing through me. "Thomas, I am getting ready to leave. You should do the same."

"Leave? And where are we going?"

"Home," I told him with a smile.

After tidying up Jonas's tent and repacking our belongings, I was not surprised to see Jonas return. He had been away the bulk of the afternoon. His face was an odd mix of dejection and determination—

his lips formed a hard, grim line, and his eyes were tired. I continued my business, not paying him any mind.

"Well, Jonas?" Tom asked, his good hand clasping his opposite elbow and working his fingers around the joint nervously.

Jonas sighed. Although my back was turned, I could feel his eyes on me, but I paid him no heed, and instead began to lace up my boots in anticipation.

"He won't let me take any leave," Jonas answered.

I heard Tom and Betsy exhale, but I drew on the presence in my stomach and kept at my tasks. The other three remained silent. I wheeled around to face them.

"So?" I asked, hands on my hips.

Tom was sitting with his head in his hand. Betsy was standing in the corner of the tent, staring at the dirt floor. Jonas alone met my gaze, and he seemed to draw on my fortitude. As we stared at each other, the dejection seemed to flee from him; he had drawn on presence as well, and in his mind a plan was forming. At length he broke the shimmering, strengthening eye contact.

"We're leaving at nightfall," he said. "Be ready."

The warm, strong feeling in my core exploded into ironclad peace. We were going, and Jonas was coming with us. I was right. Peace and purpose had won.

Betsy and I lay fully dressed on Jonas's cot atop the blankets. He'd instructed us to try and rest before we left, and we were doing our best to obey his wishes but were understandably restless. My sister fretted and fussed beside me—that was Betsy's way, of course. She was a true servant at heart and trusted authority in a way only a child could, but she could worry a body to death. I, on the other hand, was calmer. Moreover, I was letting go of the mess I'd made with Jonas. Most of my anxiety throughout the past weeks was bound up in the farm and our future. But a smaller part was reluctant to chase

Jonas because of how we'd left things—how I had ruined things. But now, since peace had laid hold of me, I found myself allowing it to extend to my heart as well as my head. Worries about Norrington were swept away, as well as my guilt over Jonas. His feelings toward me were unimportant compared to my family.

It was with this serenity that I passed into a calm sleep.

"Psst…Anne." Tom knelt by the cot, shaking my shoulders. "Time to go. Come on, Bets."

Betsy and I rose from the cot quietly, rubbing our eyes and getting our bearings. It was well past nightfall, closer to midnight. I rolled my hair and straightened my dress, then turned to help Betsy with hers. Jonas was curiously absent from our machinations.

"Tom, what time is it?" I asked.

He shrugged and continued rummaging through our satchel.

"Late," he whispered. "Jonas just woke me up and told me to rouse you two."

"Where is he?" Betsy asked. Her hand wringing had already begun.

"Gone to get the horses," Tom answered, hobbling over to us and handing Betsy the satchel.

A whistle sounded from outside. Excitement rose in me as I gave Betsy's hand a reassuring squeeze and crept toward the tent flap.

It was indeed late. The sky was black as pitch and the waning moon was high, throwing very little light on our endeavor. Tom led us away from the camp to a small clearing where our horses stood. Jonas was nowhere to be seen. I turned to Tom.

"Are we to meet him elsewhere?"

He shook his head wordlessly and gestured to Betsy to mount her horse. I made sure she was secure and set about attaching our satchel to her saddle, when we heard a rustle in the undergrowth. Knowing it was Jonas, I felt an unheeded tension flow away from me, and I smiled in spite of myself.

"Are you secure, Betsy?" I whispered, patting her leg.

She nodded and smiled.

"Brave girl."

Tom was already mounted, and Jonas was packing another satchel behind him, lashing it securely to the saddle. When he finished, he strode over to me.

"Let's go, Anne," he whispered.

"Do you not have a horse?" I asked, a little alarmed.

He shook his head shortly and bent over, clasping his hands to assist my mount.

I closed my eyes and uttered a silent prayer to God, placing my foot—and indeed my life—in Jonas's hands. Hefting me onto the horse with ease, he quickly mounted behind me, taking the reins in one hand and my waist in the other. I took several deep breaths to calm myself, wrapping my hands around the pommel and squirming to get comfortable. Jonas braced his chest against my back.

"Ready?" he whispered.

"Yes, definitely."

"I was speaking to Tom." He snapped the reins and set the horse at a trot.

Tom and Betsy followed us on their mounts wordlessly, as the silent camp fell away behind us.

It was prudent to stay quiet for as long as we could, as the rest of Jonas's camp was fast asleep. Jonas clearly didn't want to talk to me, so I concentrated on our surroundings, trying to determine in which direction we were heading. I wished not to think about the long trek ahead of us or what awaited us at the end of it.

An hour outside of the militia camp, the three horses spread single file onto a narrow track that hugged the Chowan River. Only now, with Betsy and Tom a safe distance behind us, could I ask Jonas the question to which I was so keen to know the answer.

"Jonas." My low tone in the silence of the forest sounded like a clanging gong. I startled myself, even.

"What?" He resettled his arm about my waist, sending a new army of shivers across my shoulders.

I took a deep breath. "You must tell me. Did you desert?"

He took his time answering. He allowed the silence to stretch and build so much I thought he either didn't hear me or had let the militia affect his manners. Finally, he heaved a great sigh and leaned forward to whisper in my ear.

"Nelson told me they couldn't spare me in the event that we were called to march north. They don't necessarily need me now. He's just trying to keep me close, so I'm thinking it's okay for me to take a week to ride up to check on my mother and my sister."

"So that's a yes."

I felt his nod behind me.

"A week? Jonas, it took us ten days just to ride down here."

He scoffed. "You took the long way, Anne. Tom told me how you all got turned around."

I squirmed against him, wriggling away. "Well, that was Betsy's fault, not mine."

His grasp tightened, and his voice finally held a hint of humor. "Where do you think you're wriggling, miss? Would you like me to set you down?"

I stopped my wrenching but didn't answer.

Jonas chuckled. "And since when do you listen to Betsy?"

"I was ill, Jonas, sick with a fever for half of the trip. Don't you remember?"

He didn't answer. Whether he was recalling his forced role as my nurse the previous evening, I couldn't say.

We remained quiet for a while. I found I was getting sleepy and had a mind to close my eyes and find a way to doze, when he spoke again.

"You did take the long way, Anne, but we're also making a few stops along the road. So you know, it might take five or six days."

"Stops?"

"Yes, ma'am. It just so happens that I know some people that will be right helpful to us when we meet up with Mr. Norrington."

"I see. Friends?"

"Might call them such."

"Other soldiers?"

"Other *fools,* you mean?" Hardness lilted around the edges of his voice.

"Really, Jonas! You want to discuss that *now?*"

He didn't answer for a long time. My eyes were beginning to droop when he answered.

"*Former* soldiers, you might say."

I was startled by his sudden retort and began wavering in my seat. Jonas gripped me harder, pulling me back against his chest. His chin brushed my temple as I chased the butterflies out of my stomach.

"Former, why?" I asked.

Shrugging, he answered, "Different reasons."

Contemplating this evasive retort, I considered what kind of man would be useful in a fight, yet not useful to the militia.

"Are they safe?"

Jonas chuckled roughly. "Well, no, Anne, they ain't. Wouldn't be handy to us otherwise, would they?"

Suddenly another thought entered my head, wrecking my calm for the moment. "Will they chase you, Jonas?"

"Who?"

"Nelson's men."

He only hesitated a second. "Possibly."

It would have been gracious of me to thank him for risking his career and position for us—or rather, his mother and sister—even more so to apologize, both for our last meeting and for getting him mixed up in our muddle. But I knew that neither sentiment would suit just now. So I was quiet and eventually fell asleep—my head tucked into Jonas's neck, his arm wrapped tightly around my waist.

A lightening around the edges of my vision awoke me as the horse drew to an abrupt halt. Jonas slid out from behind me, then pulled me off the horse and deposited me onto a bed of soft, dry grass. I opened my eyes long enough to see that Tom and Betsy had dismounted as well. Jonas hobbled the horses as my siblings settled down beside me to sleep. Straining to stay awake, I continued to watch Jonas until he finished his task. Only when he dropped next to Tom did I drift off to sleep once again.

IN WHICH WE TAKE A SHORT DETOUR

After a short rest in the early morning, Jonas roused us all to continue our journey. We rode again in single file in the same arrangement. This time Jonas and I were both so tired that conversation was scarce.

With so little to occupy me other than my surroundings, I closely scrutinized the landscape. The country there was very unfamiliar to me. However, I recalled that the militia was encamped near North Carolina's Chowan River and that we were somewhere in the eastern part of the territory. In that corner of North Carolina, where it met Virginia, the terrain was relatively flat and wooded, striated with small creeks that flowed into the lacy fingers of Carolina's outer banks. Where the banks began in the piedmont, the territory was marshy and swampy—unsuitable for traveling. It was best to avoid the swamps at all costs, so Jonas had to turn us a little westward.

He had other reasons for his choices, I suspected. If his regiment followed us, they would be able to locate our horses' tracks and have no difficult time locating us on our trek. Speed was of the essence, but riding through muddy creek beds helped to cover the evidence of where we had been.

We rode until the noon sun was high in the sky and then dismounted for a rest and a quick meal. While Tom and Bets were washing and taking a swallow from the creek, Jonas took me aside, gripping my elbow with urgency. We squatted down near the underbrush where he leaned close to me. His face was lined with exhaustion but had also taken on new, rigid lines of anxiety.

"Anne," he whispered, "we're almost to my first … ah … detour."

The infamous "former soldier" friends. My eyes widened, but I couldn't decide if I should be scared, worried, or excited.

He continued, "It's no place for a lady *at all*. And though Tom is a stout lad, his physical differences will draw too much attention to him."

I grabbed Jonas's elbow tightly, my fingernails digging into the canvas of his tan coat. "So you're going alone?"

He nodded slowly. When he spoke his voice was tight. "If you keep the horses on this creek bed, you won't get lost. Stay on this track until you meet up with me again. Don't stop. Don't leave the track. Do *not* vary from this course until I come and find you. And best not mention to your brother and sister what I'm doing. The less they know, the better. Do you understand me?"

I nodded, calling on my reserve supply of courage, which was rapidly depleting.

As his eyes measured my face, he squeezed my hand briefly. "Godspeed, Annie," he whispered, standing up and pulling me with him. He started to duck into the woods, but I stayed his arm.

"How long, Jonas? How long until you find us?"

At last he grinned, the tension sliding away from him in one fluid motion. He chucked me under the chin. "If I'm lucky, I'll find you by nightfall. Be brave, Anne."

And then he was gone. We trekked single file through the muddy creek bed according to Jonas's stringent directions.

Tom and Betsy were in no humor for my shifty explanations as to Jonas's whereabouts.

"But Anne," Betsy whined, "What do you mean, he's just gone?"

I sighed and rolled my eyes. "Betsy, he simply told me he had to look into some things, and he'll meet us this evening. That's all I know. Don't you trust him?"

Betsy harrumphed but otherwise said nothing.

"What about you, Thomas?" I called behind me. "Have you grievances to air as well?"

I heard his chuckle from the rear.

"Oh, not me, Annie." The humor in his voice gladdened me, and I appreciated his flexibility even more.

We traveled thus for several hours, at times silent, at others sinking into comfortable sibling reminiscences of our happy past.

"Halloo, Anne," Thomas called from the rear.

"Yes?"

"Do you recall the day that Mother was taking Mrs. Hudgins through the farm, showing off the north pasture..."

"...trying to impress her, no doubt, so her oldest son could marry Betsy," I cut in.

"Oh, Anne!" Betsy's voice shrilled from the rear. "Stop that nonsense talk! It ain't proper!"

Tom cleared his throat. "So there was Mother in all her finery, leading Abigail Hudgins..."

"...in all *her* finery," I piped in once again.

"Will you stop that, Anne? 'Tis rude," my brother complained.

"I apologize, Thomas. Do go on."

He heaved a great sigh. "As I was sayin,' Mother was leading Mrs. Hudgins through our north pasture, no doubt singing the praises of the great prestige and breeding of the Summerton name, and there we were, Anne—"

"Yes"—this time it was Betsy who interrupted, sniffing— "there you were, indeed."

Tom and I had started to titter, just barely able to continue our reminiscence.

"There we were, Anne, sitting atop the nearest apple tree..."

"...not even *our* apple tree, Thomas. Please recall that important fact."

"True, true. It was indeed Mr. Carter's apple tree."

"There we were sitting atop the tree…" I prodded, finally willing to allow Tom to finish the story.

"Apple cores strewn about the ground, green with sickness, bemoaning our fate and the number of apples we had… well…"

"…stolen?" I supplied.

"Ah… requisitioned," Thomas finished.

"Fair enough."

Betsy was the only one present who did not find the recollection wholly amusing. "Mother was furious with you two. She was just irate at the sight you made for Abigail Hudgins. Sick, barefoot, gorging yourself on stolen apples, while Mother had tried so hard to make our farm look presentable to the neighbors." She sighed. "Patrick Hudgins was reading the law in Williamsburg and was terribly handsome, Anne."

"Oh, yes, Betsy, he was," I said, stifling a giggle.

"He would have made a fetching husband."

"Indeed, Betsy. Only…"

"Yes?"

"You'd have to be sure he liked apple pie."

Tom howled with laughter, slapping his thigh and drowning out Betsy's sour *humphs*.

As I recalled the stories from our contented youth throughout the afternoon, the feeling of comfort and security grew painful. Our mother and father, the longtime symbols of ready refuge from the world, were no longer there to provide for us. Considering the absence of my parents reminded me sharply of Norrington, the reason for our journey. The sneaking feeling of despair threatened to steal over me, even as I tried to squelch it down. But really, when surveying the facts, our situation looked bleak indeed. Norrington's men were a veritable militia in themselves—burly, brooding men who answered only to Norrington himself. True, we had right on our side—and Jonas's quick wits couldn't hurt—but when stacking each side against the other, it was plain which side had the edge. And it wasn't ours.

It was into this gloom I'd sunk when Betsy begged to stop so she could stretch her legs and answer the call of nature. I glanced about dubiously, remembering Jonas's dire warning not to stop, but I reasoned that, so long as we stayed on the creek bed and made our stop short, we couldn't err too grievously.

"Very well, Betsy," I said, "go ahead and stop."

We dismounted, tying our horses to a stout oak tree and sitting down for a quick swallow of water. Betsy wandered off to find a more private location, while Tom and I stared into space, too tired to speak. It was unfortunate for us that the heat of the day, the shady locale, and the jostling of the horseback ride would tire us so, but it did. Tom and I stretched out, drifting into a light nap. Why Betsy was gone so long we never did figure out.

We were abruptly awakened by rough voices and rougher hands.

"Let's go, lass," a raspy brogue said, while large paws handled my shoulders, hauling me up to a standing position.

I groggily opened my sleepy eyes to see Tom bandied about in a similar fashion—the sight rendered me fully awake, suddenly alert. *Where is Betsy?*

Our captors—for we soon discovered that we were being taken— were two coarse men of large build and towering height, clearly wood-dwellers. Their speech was English but with an accent that came from the north, possibly Ireland. Broad shoulders were near bursting out of worn linen shirts; breeches barely covered their knees; and tall, rough boots covered their feet, rather than the customary buckled shoe of the gentleman. They were not specifically dirty, but it was plain that the forest was their natural home. Wherever they hailed from, here they were—tying our wrists behind our backs and checking our saddlebags for weapons.

"I see three horses," the larger one gestured to our mounts, "but only two of you. Is there a third one lurking?"

We shook our heads at once.

"No, sir," Tom answered. "We buried our brother several days back. Scarlet fever."

Oh, how I loved that quick-witted brother of mine! I found it most prudent to cast my eyes to the ground in distress and adopt a cheerless posture. The large man propelled us forward, while his friend led our horses behind us. I dared not look over my shoulder for Betsy, but I hoped that she was skulking in the bushes, watching us.

Oh, LORD, please protect her, I prayed silently. *And where the devil is Jonas?*

Tom and I marched with the hulking men for several hours; it was dusk when we slowed our pace. They said naught the length of the trip, but merely trudged along—at times pulling us more swiftly. Anxiety began to build in me, not just for the safety of Jonas and Betsy, but suddenly for my own as well.

What on earth could these men want with us? Are they going to hurt us? Are Tom and I marching to our death?

I could see a faint light in the distance, emanating from a worn bungalow. As we drew closer, several cottages appeared, all clumped together in a communal circle. Voices and laughter piped out of the largest—the one with the blazing lights and the comforting smoke puffing from the bumpy chimney. The evening air was cooling, even for midsummer, and the heady smell of wood smoke and a supper cooking warmed my senses, despite not knowing our eventual fate.

The men drew us to a halt, untying our hands and shoving us forward. Not to the large happy cottage, but toward one of the small, dark ones. In truth, it could scarcely be called a cottage—shack was a more apt description. Small and barely more than a lean-to, it was not lit and promised very little comfort. It was a place of darkness and rank odor and none too inviting.

Imagine my surprise when we were not even led into this small, dirty shack, but were instead tied to a rough wood beam erected next to it. Even after so many nights of sleeping outside, I was absolutely terrified of being immobilized and left outside to the elements and the forest animals. For all my hours of stoic silence with our captors, I finally started to struggle and whimper.

"No!" I wiggled against the larger man's grasp. "No! Let me go! Don't tie me up here!" I tried to wrench my hands free from his, but of course his strength far outweighed my own—not to mention his fleshy arms that were twice the thickness of my spindly ones.

His strong hands crushed my wrists together, tying them to the pole behind me. I could feel Tom's hands, which were grasping to hold my own in a failing effort to calm me. Although the battle to get free was already lost, panic overwhelmed me, and I began to scream.

"No! Help me! Let me go!"

My appeals were cut short as the large man cuffed me across the face with his meaty fist, causing my vision to wobble and waver. Darkness clouded my head as I blacked out.

Shouts and a cool cloth brought me around, and I was pleased to find that my hands were unbound. My head ached like the devil, though. I was reclined on the ground, my head on an unknown lap, and it was pitch dark. I tried to sit up, eyes still closed, but the world swam around me as I fell back.

"Easy, Annie," Tom whispered from above. "Stay down. We're okay now. Jonas is here."

"Jonas? Here?" I tried again to sit up, but Tom pushed my shoulder down.

"Oh, yes," Tom's voice was thick with joyful amusement. "He's here, all right."

Finding that opening my eyes and sitting up was a task outside the realm of possibility, I allowed myself to relax as much as I could. At length I was swept up in somebody's arms. My injured head bobbed uncomfortably, and a soft gasp of pain escaped me. Whoever held me grasped me tighter. I opened my eyes and could barely make out Jonas's face in the firelight from the large cabin toward which we were swiftly moving.

"Jonas," I whispered.

"I'm here."

"Ow. My head hurts."

A muscle flickered near his jaw. "Yes, I know. I cannot believe he struck you. We will have words about that."

Panic fluttered in my chest again; the prospect of Jonas having an altercation with the large, burly man was not appealing. "No, don't," I argued weakly, letting my head drop against his shoulder. "They are huge, dangerous men. They'll harm you."

Jonas threw his head back and laughed. "Douglas is not going to hurt me, Anne. Don't you fret about that."

"You know these men?"

He chuckled. "You could say that."

We had reached the large, welcoming cabin. The main room was fitted with a large dining table, a cooking fire, and a narrow bed. It was clean and smelled smoky and wonderfully inviting. In the corner there was a ladder to a loft, I supposed. Jonas quickly deposited me onto the bed, which was surprisingly soft. My worn body seemed to melt into it.

A woman of similar bulky build and woodsy clothing came and tended to me immediately. She had soft red hair, split into two long plaits, and shining, clear skin. Her blue eyes held the glow of merriness but were now narrowed in concern.

"Greta, this is Anne." Jonas waved his hand toward me dismissively. "Will you see to her wound?" He strode to the doorway where Tom and the larger man were looming.

After a few whispered words of conference, Tom slipped quietly out of the house.

Greta glanced over my face and clucked her tongue. "Aye, he did an ill turn to you, miss, cuffing you like that. Douglas don't know how to handle a screaming lass. I'm right sorry he hit you, and that's the truth."

I nodded weakly, trying to smile.

"I'm pleased to meet you, Miss Anne," she said. Greta busied herself with a vinegar-soaked rag, wiping my face and tenderly dabbing the now swollen area of my temple where Douglas so unceremoniously struck me.

A stinging pain shot through me as she touched it. I yelped, causing both Jonas and Douglas to jump in surprise in the corner where they stood. Greta glanced their way, and we both caught the dark look pass between them.

"Truth is," she whispered as she leaned over me, "Mr. Jonas was right angry when he saw you laid out and bleeding in the yard. Douglas would never have took you had he known you were his girl."

"I am *not* Jonas's girl," I said.

Greta eyed me. "Have it your way, miss." She brushed my hair back from my face and rearranged the pillow behind my head. "There. All better now?"

"A little." Greta's skill as a nursemaid reminded me of my lost sister, Betsy. I panicked and shot up in the bed, screeching toward the men huddled in the corner. "Jonas! Come here! We need Betsy! She..."

Jonas rushed over to my side and knelt next to the bed. "Easy there, Anne." He eased me back onto the bed. "Don't upset yourself." As he leaned over me and searched my face, a trace of worry crossed his brow. He gently probed the knot at my temple. "How's your head? It still *feels* fairly hard—what a relief to know you'll be as stubborn as always."

I tried to manage a smile. "Jonas, when your, um, *friends* took us, Betsy was still in the woods."

He nodded quickly. "Yes, I know. Douglas's son, James, has gone back to fetch her. Tom went with him so Betsy wouldn't be frightened."

That was reassuring. I couldn't imagine how Betsy had fared all day in the woods alone, wondering what had become of Tom and me.

She would probably worry and nag those poor men all the way back here to the cottage. The thought made me grin.

"What makes you smile so?" Jonas asked, sitting on the edge of the bed.

"Those men are no match for Betsy," I answered with false gravity—my mouth trembling with unshed mirth.

"Indeed, and I do not envy them," he said with a smirk.

We smiled in conspiratorial silence.

After a moment I tried to rise up to my elbows; I managed with Jonas's assistance. "Jonas," I said, my voice turning businesslike, "I have several questions I need you to answer."

His eyebrows shot up in amusement. "Well, go on ahead, m'lady." He gestured with his hand in mock subservience.

"How do you know these men?"

Jonas's countenance immediately turned mysterious. "Ah, well, let's just say that Douglas ran afoul of his regimental leader in the militia, and I helped him out of his difficulty. The rest of them here are Douglas's family and extended family, all from Scotland. Greta is his wife, James is his son, and Sean—your other escort—is Douglas's brother. They're good men, Anne. I know they gave you and Tom a scare, and your head there is even worse, but they didn't mean harm to you personally."

"Were you coming to them today when you left us in the clearing?"

He nodded, no further explanation forthcoming.

"Why didn't you want to bring us with you? They seem friendly enough, now that you're here."

Jonas paused before answering me, weighing his words. "Anne, they are good people, but they are outlaws in their way. The less you and your family are acquainted with them, the better."

I shifted on the bed, feeling stiff but still unwilling to move my head too much lest the shocks of pain assault me again.

"Anything else?" Jonas asked, making to take his leave from my bedside.

"Is it so unsightly?" I gestured to the bruise on my head.

He pursed his lips and cocked his head, running a callused finger around my injury. "It'll heal up, Anne. And you'll still be pleasant to look upon."

Jonas's plan, such as it was, never included us remaining with his friends overnight—I would wager that Jonas's plans never included us even *meeting* the McLean family—but Greta insisted that I was not fit to be moved until I had rested well in her bed. That night Jonas, Tom, Douglas, James, Sean, and a few extended cousins, stayed outside by the fire and talked of their plans well past moonrise. Betsy had returned hours before and was equally fussed over and tended to by Greta.

The reunion between sisters was poignant with enough weeping and squealing to cause the men to exit the cabin at once. Happily, Betsy, for her hours of solitude in the forest, was no worse for wear. She had heard the men coming from her perch beneath a rhododendron tree and had stayed still throughout the discussion of our leave taking. After watching Douglas and James lead us away, she had crept back to the main path and stayed put until Tom came back for her.

"I know I'm not usually brave, Anne," she whispered later that evening while we were tucked into Greta's bed—the men still at their strategizing outside. "But somehow I knew it would be well, and that you, Tom, or Jonas would be back directly." She sighed, rolling her violet eyes in my direction. "Is that strange?"

"No, Bets. I think it's very clever of you. To be sure, when I awoke and heard that Tom had gone to fetch you, I was very relieved."

She squeezed my hand. "What do you think we'll do now, Anne?"

I shrugged in the well-insulated softness of the bed. "I don't know."

"Well, one thing is for certain," she said.

"What is that?"

She shook her head at me. "We must cover that bruise until it's healed. It's hideous, Anne. Do you not have a serviceable bonnet?"

Turns out that the McLean family was plenty willing to angle for a fight on our behalf. Douglas told Jonas he had heard of Norrington even this far south and was eager to bring his family up to Abbingdon to teach him a lesson—especially since, in his words, "We've not had a good ruckus since we were booted out of the militia."

However, as our group was only eight strong, including the McLeans, Douglas thought we could use more manpower. That's what the late night parlay was all about—while Bets and I slept soundly in the cabin. The village of Corapeake was about a day's ride from the McLean homestead, and there lived a sizeable family of the McLean's acquaintance. We were informed at breakfast that we would ride there directly to meet with the men in question and request their aid.

There was something else to this plan—*that* I could plainly see. All of my inquiries about the deeper nature of the next phase of our plan were met with assured smiles and condescending jokes. Clearly, Jonas was holding his cards close to his chest. As we rode out the next morning—this time alone on my mount, Jonas having acquired one from Douglas—I secretly watched the thoughts and plans making war on his countenance.

Douglas drew next to me so that Jonas could make his escape from my queries. "He's a quiet one, is Jonas. You'll not get a mite of information out of him that he doesn't want to share."

"So I see," I murmured.

My companion rubbed his chin thoughtfully, casting a contrite glance in my direction. "Miss Summerton, I'm very sorry for the blow I dealt you last night. I see it has marred your pretty face, and I feel terrible about it."

I smiled at him in response. "That's quite all right, Douglas. Thank you—I accept your apology. And thank you for accompanying us."

The big man boomed with laughter. "Oh, I'd do even more for my friend Jonas, miss. Depend upon that. I could tell you many a tale about him."

Jonas, who had fallen back to hear our conversation, drew rein next to me. "That's enough, Douglas," he said gruffly. "Miss Anne doesn't *need* to hear any tales."

Douglas grinned, blue eyes twinkling, and spurred his horse ahead. I threw a sidelong glance in Jonas's direction, raising my eyebrows inquisitively. Jonas ignored me. I would get no more information today.

Even Tom, my advocate, would tell me nothing. "Best not to ask, Annie," was all he would say.

And so we rode on to Corapeake and whatever God had in store for us there.

IN WHICH WE ATTEND
THE LOCAL FESTIVITIES

Our destination—the village of Corapeake—sat very near the border between Virginia and North Carolina. It wasn't much of a village to speak of. What little distinction it bore was related more to the Campbell clan and their impact in the county.

Much to my delight, Douglas saw fit tell me all about the Campbells, a large family—*very* large—also from Scotland. Their patriarch, Logan, was quite the county man—involved in several aspects of town politics and quite outspoken against the British. Indeed, he seemed to have his finger in all facets of Gates county business. The Campbells lived on an enormous parcel of land outside of the village. Logan was well connected with the state militia and had many friends in important circles.

The ride to Corpeake was well peppered with diverting conversation.

"So you see, Miss Anne," Douglas said, leaning across the track to engage me privately, "the Campbells are an excellent lot to have on our side. And Captain Jonas, well, he knows that. So off we ride to speak to their master. He'll be no friend to a Tory rogue bullying about young widows and misses, so I think we've a fair chance of success." Leaning back to his own space on his mount, he chuckled heartily, drawing the attention of our fellow riders. "Yes, that's right. Ought to be quite a scrap up in Abbingdon, hey, Jonas?"

Jonas, who was riding about twenty feet ahead of us but listening all the same, threw a look of barely patient indulgence over his shoulder at Douglas. He said nothing, which encouraged Douglas's roars all the more.

"So, Douglas," I whispered, not wishing to draw Jonas's attention to my inquiries. He had been so tight-lipped since we left the McLean family housing that I was plainly *dying* to find out some useful information. "Where exactly are we *going* to see the Campbells?"

"Oh, well, it's midsummer, as you know, Miss Anne, and the Campbells will be out on their land having a feast. Yes, miss, a grand old feast—the likes of which you've never seen or yet will see again."

"A feast for midsummer?" I asked.

Douglas's bushy eyebrows rose, surprised at my ignorance. "Why, yes, it's an old Celtic ritual to ask the gods to bless the coming harvest."

"Pagans." Jonas's mutter was barely discernible.

Covering my snicker, I returned my attention to Douglas. "At these feasts, do they perform, um, rituals?"

Douglas roared once again with thundering laughter, enough to wake the nymphs from the neighboring trees. "Oh, no, Miss Anne, they're not so serious Celtics as all that. They dance and eat and drink lots of ale and sing songs—and late into the night they tell stories about the old Celtic gods."

"Lots and lots of ale," Jonas added.

Douglas nodded. "Aye, that is so, and Midsummer with the Campbells is as raucous an eve as you'll ever see, Miss Anne. Just mark my words."

"It sounds like a whole heap of fun to me!" Tom rejoined from behind me. "Point me to the ale, Mr. Douglas!"

"Aye, I do like the way you think, young Tom!" Douglas said. "Now, Miss Anne, I'll need to warn you and Miss Betsy to stay close to your own men. The Campbells are friendly enough, but a feast is a feast, and I have seen things turn a little wild."

To me that sounded just right. After the drudgery of the preceding months, some wild amusement was exactly what I needed.

Douglas and Jonas led us to a wide clearing, wide enough for our own horses and tents. The men had packed the camping supplies on the last beast, so when it arrived they bustled about setting up our dwellings and locating an appropriate spot for a fire.

"Anne, Betsy, go and gather some firewood. And don't stray too far, you hear?" Jonas called over his shoulder, struggling with the ropes on the packhorse. "As much as you can carry."

Betsy, who was almost too tired to stand, glanced at me wearily. I squeezed her shoulders in a brief hug, feeling generous and in need of a short ramble. "Take a rest, Bets, I'll go get the timber."

I started off into the wood, watching carefully behind me to be sure I could find my way back to the camp. Firewood was plentiful, and I scampered about, pulling as many handfuls as I could into my arms. The branches left soggy dirt streaks on my dress as I held them. With despair I glanced at it and almost wished for the wedding clothes Mrs. Wilkins had promised before my wedding to Nate. Greta McLean had washed our spare dresses the day before, and now this one was hopelessly dirty. Hauling wood against my skirts would not aid the situation at all. When my arms were full, I stood up straight with my firewood and looked around for the way back to the campsite.

Alarmingly, I could not for my life recognize the clearing in which I stood.

"Oh, of course. I *would* get lost out here. That's just my way."

Now I wasn't completely lost; after all, I'd only been away from camp for ten minutes or less, so I couldn't be that far away. And yet the boxwood bushes I had pushed aside as I left our clearing were nowhere to be seen. What to do? Staying put was really the best option. If I wandered about, I would just get more lost and tired to boot. Yes, it would be best to stay still.

I stood on my spot, arms full of wood, for close on five minutes before I began to wish I were back with my friends and family. At length I just decided to scream.

"Tom! Betsy! Jonas!" I belted at the top of my voice. Almost immediately I heard voices at my rear—not at all in the area I'd surmised was the correct path. Oh, well.

"Anne! Where are you?" Jonas's voice was growing somewhat closer.

"Over here!" I stayed still, not wanting to move in the incorrect direction.

Finally he burst through the bushes, looking at once exasperated and relieved. "There you are." He huffed, catching his breath. "Anne, can't you even stray a few feet from camp without getting lost?" He took the wood from my arms, glancing about. "Where's Betsy?"

"She looked so tired I told her to stay behind."

He narrowed his eyes at me. "Anne, none of us need wander about alone, do you hear me? It's not safe. You should already be aware of that."

I said nothing, too frustrated to speak. There was no outlet for my exasperation anyway. Who could I blame for this uncomfortable, unsafe, unsavory situation? Not a one, not even myself, for I was forced to come here by Norrington's untimely ultimatum. I bent down to retrieve more firewood so we could carry out twice as much. Jonas just watched me silently.

When I finished my task, I stood erect and stared blankly at him and flatly said, "Well, lead me out, Mr. Blake." The corner of Jonas's mouth twitched slightly. He led me through the woods to our clearing—where, amazingly, half a dozen tents had been erected and a fire pit cleared at their center.

Jonas glanced at me over his shoulder. "I believe Douglas has a surprise for you and Betsy."

"A surprise?" I dumped the wood by the fire pit unceremoniously and sought after my sister.

"Bets? Where are you?" I called.

"In here, Anne!" she answered from the nearest tent. I pulled up the flap and found her surrounded by gowns—a small, open trunk at her feet. A yellow muslin was spread on the bed; she held another blue calico up to her neck.

"Oh, Anne, aren't they lovely? Douglas said we could each pick two new gowns from this trunk—to keep! Can you imagine? Anne, we haven't had new gowns in an *age!*"

Betsy was right, and although the gowns were not perfectly new, they were new to us, and I was readily pleased.

Jonas stirred beside me in the open tent flap. "What do you ladies think?" he asked with a smile.

My beautiful sister didn't hear him for all of her twirling and preening in the small space. Muffling a chuckle, I turned to Jonas. "Ah ... I *think* she is pleased."

"And you?"

I let the question hang for a moment; to own the truth, I was more pleased that Jonas sought my opinion. Eventually I nodded and smiled. "I will choose a couple for myself."

Jonas inclined his head. "The Campbell's midsummer fair is a good place for you and Betsy to go out and enjoy yourselves. I understand that much time has passed since you girls saw a party."

"I believe Father's barn raising was the last joyous event in my recent memory."

The silence hung thick in the tent, broken only by Betsy's continued squeaks and squeals.

Arching an eyebrow, I turned to Jonas and smiled. "And where did Douglas come by such lovely gowns?"

He simply shrugged, smirking just a bit. "It's always best not to ask, Anne."

When dusk began to tinge the sky with a fair pink, ushering in a cool breeze that stirred the leaves, we set out on horseback to the Campbell farm. Douglas informed us that it was "naught but a hair's breadth away," but as usual, I was skeptical of everything Douglas said. Betsy was beautifully outfitted in the blue calico—the sleeves widened out at her elbows, and the lace above her stomacher was starched and nearly white. It really was a much nicer gown than any we owned, and I was happy to see her looking so pretty and excited. In addition to a pale pink cambric gown that was carefully wrapped among my things in my tent, I had chosen an apple-green frock that sent Betsy into fits.

"It's not a great hue for me, Anne," she had said. "But it looks very lovely on you."

No matter how it looked on me, I was glad to have it. It flattered my thin frame, added some color to my sallow cheeks, and complimented my flaxen hair—if I could say so myself. In general, our entire party was in high spirits as we rode single file through the forest to the Campbell farm.

After another quarter hour we heard music and saw fires blazing through the trees ahead. The music was quite unlike anything that had ever reached my ears. Not that I had ever graced the drawing rooms of Williamsburg or Richmond, but I was familiar with several of the popular dancing melodies of the day. However, the music I heard that evening was like a fairy's song—light and airy, employing various stringed instruments and rhythmic, pounding drums. My foot immediately began to tap in my stirrup.

"Ah, Miss Anne, you'll have to wait but a few moments longer before you begin to dance!" Douglas commented upon seeing my excitement. "Did I not tell you it was a sight to behold?"

And it was. As we broke through the last line of trees, I could barely steer my mare for amazement at the scene before me. The Campbell clan had a piece of land as far as I could see, with homes and cottages spread throughout. A large number of dwellings were prettily grouped in a semicircle of sorts, with the land in between utilized for this evening's events. I counted four lit bonfires. At least a dozen tables lay about, each laden with a bounty of food. Ropes of small lanterns were draped among the trees. Each fire was encircled by a ring of dancers, grouped in pairs, twirling about each other and around the fire at the same time. My breath caught in my throat. I had no wish to dance; just to sit and watch them was plenty exciting.

Tom broke my attentive reverie. Having led my horse to the stable door while I was gazing, he waited to assist my dismount.

"Come, Annie." His good arm was outstretched.

I reached down for it, but Jonas interrupted us.

"No need to do that, Tom. Let me." Jonas quickly took my open hand and grasped me about the waist, lifting me from my horse. Just as quickly he deposited me on the ground, dropping my hand and turning away. The whole incident was swift and awkward somehow, but glancing at Tom I could see his relief. I was reminded how difficult the riding and camping must be on his limbs.

"Well, at least let me walk her to the party, Jonas," Tom said, holding out his arm.

"Thank you, Jonas," I said, taking Tom's arm and walking with heightened expectations into the darkening night.

Betsy walked behind us with Douglas's brother. James McLean seemed plenty kind but hadn't near as much to say as his older brother, who was bringing up our rear.

As our party entered the circle of light, Jonas and Douglas immediately became serious about their task, glancing about the gathering furtively for Logan Campbell. Betsy, Tom, James, and I wandered to a table laden with food, as we had not eaten a solidly good meal since we left the McLean cabin that morning. Betsy and I attempted to eat as daintily as possible but failed miserably—for our appetites were hardy, and it showed. James left for a few moments, returning with four mugs of ale. The sweet amber liquid had some bite to it, but otherwise I'd tasted nothing so refreshing.

Betsy, however, was displaying a bit of shock.

"Anne, do you really think you ought to drink the ale?" she whispered, gesturing to her mug with unease. "I mean, it's not quite ladylike, don't you think?"

Tom stared at her and shook his head with a smirk.

However, it was I who answered with as much patience as I could manage. "Betsy, do tell me exactly how many ladylike things we have done in the past two weeks. Spent two nights in a militia camp. Rode through the state of North Carolina with a deserter. Stayed with a family of outlaws in their house in the woods. And your dress—do you think it was come by through honest means?"

At this Betsy gaped. Whatever improper wrongs must be righted, let them not include the new frocks!

I continued, "What of those events have been entirely ladylike, I ask you?"

I wasn't sure how Betsy would react to my outburst. Tom and I watched her closely, and I noticed that James had also leaned forward to view the performance. However, to the delight of us all, a wide grin broke across her pretty face, and she began to cackle merrily. To that end, we all joined in, crashing our mugs together and drinking more ale.

At length I glanced about the party and noted that Jonas and Douglas were seated beside an older gentleman at the edge of the next fire. *He must be the patriarch, Logan Campbell,* I thought, because he looked every bit the distinguished and powerful gentleman of the county. His auburn hair, which he wore loose, was streaked with gray—the effect of the two colors mixed was striking. He was taller than both Jonas and Douglas, which is saying much, and was powerfully built, broad, and strong. An air of authority and respect surrounded him like a tartan cloak. I must say, I feared him immediately.

The three men were locked in deep conversation, but the general appearance of the dialogue looked agreeable. A small flutter persisted in my abdomen as I watched them. Only James, who was nudging my elbow with a fresh mug of ale, eventually distracted me. I accepted the drink gratefully as the four of us meandered to a hay bale set closer to the fire. Lively banter, merry laughter, and energetic dancing surrounded us. There was a florid mix of conversation and music—color and motion that, along with the ale, assaulted my senses pleasantly. The music grew to a pitch, along with my excitement. I drank my ale, leaned my head back against the hay, and smiled gratefully to the heavens, tapping my foot to the pulse of the song.

This, God, I thought, *this is wonderful. Thank you.*

The firelight was bright around me, but the midsummer sky was darkening quickly; stars were appearing, stark and shiny white against a dark blue backdrop. As I sat, the music pounding its ethereal rhythm into my head, the tension began to fall away from me in waves.

Or perhaps it was the ale.

The next thing I knew, James had pulled Betsy up by the elbows and was spinning her about in the dance. Tom and I hooted with delight as we watched our buttoned-up sister twirled around the fire by the Scots-born outlaw. What hilarity was before us, and what our parents would say if they could see her! Betsy was enjoying herself heartily, a gleeful smile playing on her pretty face. It looked so entertaining I grew a bit envious, but I couldn't let Tom see, so I continued to laugh at his jokes and watch Betsy.

As that song ended and another took its place, James deposited Betsy next to us and held his arm out to me. "Come, Miss Anne. It's your turn!"

I assented readily. Soon I, too, was twirling about the fire—my hands clasped in James's large ones, the wind whipping my hair out of its knot. It was as sublime a moment as I'd known in years.

Jonas appeared next to us, ready to take me in his arms for his turn about the fire. "Come, James, we must share the Summerton girls! Go and take Betsy for another spin!"

James gave me up with smiling goodwill. And so Jonas and I began our revolution, feet skipping sideways, hands clasped on each other's arms—the both of us laughing so hard we could barely keep the beat of the music. The song slowed to its end, only to have another begin again, and so Jonas and I picked up our skipping pace with the rest of the dancers. Occasionally, he would lay his hand on my waist and twirl me in a circle as we were skipping, but it required several attempts to perfect that movement. We didn't speak. We simply forgot all present fears and complications.

At the end of the second song, Jonas led me by the hand to an empty hay bale away from the fire, for we were heated from our dance. It was fairly separated from the crowd, situated at the end of a small wood at the north end of the Campbell property. He sat me down and walked away, only to reappear moments later with a mug of strong tea.

"Enough ale for you, Miss Anne," he said with a slight smirk.

I said nothing, but moved aside so he could join me on my perch. My heart had just slowed its rapid pounding from the dance and the proximity to Jonas. To clear my mind of its tangled thoughts, I broached the topic of Logan Campbell. "So?" I waited for him to speak.

"So ... what?"

"So I saw you talking to Mr. Campbell. What did he say?"

"Ah, yes ... Mr. Campbell." Jonas leaned forward and put his head in his hands, and for the first time, I could see that he, too, was tired and fearful and possibly—just possibly—slightly vulnerable.

I waited quietly at his side.

After a few silent moments, he lifted his head. "Mr. Campbell is inclined to join us but would like to speak to his fellow clansmen later this evening—when the sharing and storytelling begins."

Later ... and just how late was later? I wanted to know. The ale had made me sleepy enough.

"I know," he said, patting my hand. "We shall need to wait, Anne. We'll find a quiet place for you and Betsy to rest until the dancing subsides."

I didn't answer, instead thinking of Mr. Campbell and all of his family and friends who could ride into Virginia to help us. Surely a man with his influence and authority wouldn't hesitate to lend us some powerful aid.

"Anne?" Jonas interrupted my thoughts.

"Hmm?"

"You look quite lovely in that new frock."

"Thank you, Jonas. You know—"

I was interrupted by some shouts from the nearest fire and rapid hoof beats making their way across the clearing. A cold chill made its way up my back; the stable was in the opposite direction.

I dug my fingers into Jonas's arm. "Who is riding through the clearing without stabling their mounts, Jonas?"

Jonas did not answer but was staring into the darkness, as if by narrowing his eyes he could stare away the dark to determine who the intruders were. I decided my best course of action was to remain still and seated next to him. Should danger be afoot, I was loath to be in this wide space alone.

A branch crackled next to us. We whipped about, tension locking our limbs, but it was only James McLean. He grasped Jonas roughly by the shoulder. "Jonas, they are men from Nelson's militia. They're shouting about the fires looking for you. Best run now. Now, Jonas! My father says to go. We'll tend to the Summertons."

Jonas's eyes widened; his mouth was hard with determination. He grasped my hand and pulled me along swiftly—away from the fires, the crowds, the gay laughter, and the approaching horsemen.

"Wait! Jonas! Where are we going? Where are you taking me?" I yanked my arm free. As frightened as I was for him, I was equally as frightened to lose myself in the woods once again.

"I am *not* leaving you here. Now come along, Anne." He slid his arm around my waist and pulled me with him into the darkening wood, Nelson's militia following rapidly behind us.

IN WHICH I LEARN OF HORTICULTURE

We scurried along for half of an hour or more—not speaking, tearing through bushes and ducking under low tree limbs. I tried in vain not to think about what this little stroll was doing to my new gown.

And all along the hoof beats continued to sound around us—at times close enough to make me catch my breath, at others farther away. Even worse, we did not yet know if any men were following on foot. I was fully and completely frightened by this time, but Jonas showed no signs of wear or fear. He continued to plod through the forest, holding firmly to my hand or arm, helping me through the rough spots on our trek.

I was growing weary with stress and fatigue when we heard voices alarmingly close. Jonas stopped, glancing about furtively. His eyes focused on a low hedgerow at our feet, and I saw the split decision flash across his face.

Oh, no, I thought warily. *Not the bushes.*

He put his hands on my shoulders. "Now, Anne, you're going to have to trust me," he whispered.

I nodded, beginning to shake in fear as the voices grew louder. Jonas gave me a hard shove, forcing my body down to the ground.

He squatted down next to me. "Now, roll under the bush."

I did as I was bid and was surprised to find a fair bit of room under there. To be sure, a few low-lying branches poked me, but I was lying comfortably and well out of sight. Jonas bent down until he could see me.

"Stay still and quiet. I'll be back soon." He departed without ceremony, leaving me in the underbrush.

Now that I was well hidden, I found little cause to fear. It was dark, after all, and with such a thick cover of foliage over my head, I would surely go unnoticed by the militia. *And really, they aren't looking for me anyway,* I thought. *They're after Jonas.* As comforting as the thought was, it was a false comfort, as his being caught and detained carried its own set of problems. My mind couldn't bear to contemplate what they would possibly do to him. Certainly we couldn't stand to lose him; he was too crucial to keeping peace among the motley crew we called our support. I had difficulty seeing past our marching into Abbingdon without his cool head and firm hand to guide us.

Which brought me to my next thought: what were Tom, Betsy, and I to do during the altercation if it came to a fight? Supposing Tom could help out somehow, surely Betsy and I didn't need to be there in the thick of it. That would be dangerous, first off; and besides, if it came to deathblows, I couldn't square with being the one to order the killing of Will Norrington. And yet … to be sequestered in my home by the men, forced to hear of the action second hand? That didn't sit well with me either. My inability to decide exactly *where* I wanted to be during the fight was frustrating.

So that was a dilemma to ponder, and it consumed the space of time it took for Jonas to create a false trail for the militia to follow.

At length he appeared before me, peering under the bushes. "Hey, Anne," he whispered with a spirited grin.

"What are you so satisfied about?" After all, he was not the one crammed beneath the foliage for such a lengthy space of time.

"I think I led them out of the woods. And what of you? Do you wish to come out of there or not, missy?"

He extended his hand, and I was placing mine in it when we heard a gunshot. Chills extended throughout my cramped body.

Jonas squatted down and launched himself into the bush next to me. There was barely room for him.

"What are you doing? Get out of here! You go find your own bush!"

Jonas responded by clamping his hand over my mouth.

I could see that his shoulder clearly extended past the edge of the bush. If someone happened to look down, they would see him. I scooted inward, trying to wedge my body on its side to give him more room; he followed suit, and within seconds both of us were completely underneath the growth. However, we were also extremely cramped. My head was locked under Jonas's chin, and our bodies were awkwardly pressed together. But by far the meanest insult was his hand, still covering my mouth as if I was a child. I wriggled my head to get free.

"Who was that?" I whispered.

He just barely shook his head in response, a movement I could feel by his stubbled chin scraping against my forehead. Jonas let his arm fall across my back protectively in an awkward embrace but otherwise said nothing. We stayed quite still for a long while. I knew it was no use to speak, as he was listening intently to the night sounds. I couldn't hear anything in particular, but I nearly burst my ears trying. It must have been twenty or thirty minutes before I ventured to have a word.

"Jonas?" I whispered into his collarbone, trying to tilt my head upward.

"Mmm?" his voice was muffled.

"Is it safe for us to go now?"

His entire body was tense, listening for further sounds of pursuit. I myself hadn't heard a darn thing since the gunshot.

"Well?"

"Shh…"

I rolled my eyes and wiggled to stretch my immobile muscles. My arms were curved in front of me, sandwiched against Jonas, who had managed to fit one of his arms over me and one under his head. That was wholly unfair! He looked almost comfortable!

As if reading my mind, he whispered, "Are you comfortable, Anne?"

I snorted in the dark stillness. "Surely you jest. How could I be?"

He chuckled quietly. "I'm waiting for the moon to pass, and then I'll go out and have a look around. Not long now. Here, see if you can get an arm free."

He lifted his arm off of my waist, leaving me a small amount of room. I wiggled my arm out and threaded it through the space he left, letting it drop behind his back. His arm resumed its place at my hip. I was trying not to think about that.

"Better?"

"I suppose."

He sighed. "I'm sorry. I know this is awkward."

"You could say that."

He snickered softly. "Direct, aren't you? You're a far cry from the girl I knew two years ago."

Not knowing if this was a criticism or a compliment, I elected not to respond.

Since this attempt at conversation failed, we lapsed back into uncomfortable silence. The forced intimacy of travel and illness, not to mention the near crisis at our homestead, was stalling the restoration of our friendship. There were simply too many other things going on.

After another lengthy silence, Jonas removed his arm from around me and wiggled, back first, out from under the hedge. Before resuming his feet, he paused for a few moments, continuing to listen; then he reached in, squeezed my hand, and crept away. As pleasing as it was to stretch out, I found it quite lonely and a little frightening without him. After all, it had grown very late and well past the time I should be asleep. Just the thought of sleep, even in a worn tent with only Betsy and no furniture to speak of, made me undeniably tired, and I closed my eyes.

How long I was asleep, I couldn't say. But I awoke with a start when Jonas reached beneath the shrub to take my arm. There was a swift moment of terror when I found myself under a bush with an assortment of branches lodged into my back, and I cried out. Jonas quickly gripped my shoulders and at once pulled me from my long-standing hiding place, the branches gouging my face and arms in the process.

"Anne! Hush! You are safe!" Pulling me into his arms to silence me, Jonas whispered in my ear, "You must be quiet!" He pressed my head to his shoulder, holding me close until I was composed.

It took me several moments to gain my surroundings, but when I was fully cognizant, I recalled our evening in the hedgerow and calmed down. Then there was the issue of the sharp pains in my limbs from their inactivity and the many bleeding scrapes on my face and arms from my hasty exit. Jonas led me by the hand to a nearby stream where he used my handkerchief to dab the blood from my face.

"Poor, Anne," he said. "You've had it rough these past two days, haven't you?"

I nodded dully, too fatigued to consider rational conversation.

"Are you well? Do you have any other pains?"

I stretched my legs and arms to take stock—they were fine beyond being stiff. The scratches on my cheeks and forearms stung, but they would heal. The knot on my temple, still a light blue tinge, was much less painful than it had been the previous day. So all in all, I believed I would survive.

"I'm fine," I whispered, heaving myself off the rock where we sat.

Jonas followed suit and, offering me his arm, began to lead us through the woods to our camp.

The moon had passed; in fact, it was little to be seen under our deep cover. Although my injuries were slight, I found myself exhausted, which made the walking difficult.

"How far are we from our camp?" I asked wearily, after a few minutes of tiring travel.

Jonas hesitated. "A while yet. Are you unwell?"

"No." I sighed. "Just very, very tired. It must be quite late."

He nodded. "Still a few hours before dawn."

I groaned. "By the time we arrive at camp, it will be time to mount up and ride for Abbingdon, will it not?"

Jonas didn't answer, which was not encouraging. The trek through the forest was wreaking havoc on my feet, which somehow couldn't manage the logs and branches.

"You appear to have trouble walking. Shall I *carry* you?" Jonas asked.

I glared at him through the moonlight. "I am quite well, thank you. But perhaps you could tell me a good story to keep me awake."

"A story?" His blue eyes widened in surprise. "You are the novel reader, Anne, not I."

"True, but you are the one who has traveled with the militia for two years. You could tell me, for instance, how you came to be in such power over the McLean family."

Cocking his head, he said, "Oh, I wouldn't call it *power*."

I snorted. "Control?"

Jonas rubbed his chin thoughtfully. "How about *influence?*"

"Very well, then. Influence. Begin your story, please."

"At your service, miss! It happened like this . . ."

"Douglas and his boys, see, they're not what you'd call *Virginians* strictly. That is to say, they kind of live wherever they can. Their place is clearly in North Carolina now, but eighteen months back the property line was, well, indistinct. So, Anne, these boys, they're not exactly law-abiding, but not general criminals either—a fact you have probably discerned already. But when the word came that they were training up militias, and that good soldiers might even get sent up to General Washington's army, well, Douglas and his boys signed up straight away.

"Yes, I said *boys*. You have met James, and he is the best of the lot. But there is also Charles (Charlie, really) and William (Billy to all of his friends). Douglas also has a daughter, I've heard, but I have yet to meet her, so I really can't be sure.

"Anyway, Douglas and his boys were training in the Virginia militia with me, before I got sent up to Nelson's outfit. And our captain, he was an unwholesome, unsavory fellow, and I will leave it at that. A real bell swagger. Rollins, his name was, and he took no liking to the McLean boys. Said Scotsmen reminded him too much of the English, and he couldn't abide by the English. So really, instead of training those boys as he should have been, Rollins just set to making their lives miserable. All of the worst jobs at the camp fell to the McLeans, and those of us in training weren't allowed to say or do anything about it."

"Why not?"

"Why? Because, Anne, an army is built on discipline and obedience. If you can't trust your men to do as you say in a safe training camp, how can you trust them when the lobster-backs are breathing down your necks?"

I found that the spirited debate was doing much to improve my mood. "That seems counterproductive, Jonas. Not at all an effective means of generating trust among your men!"

"No, Anne, listen. You can't tolerate disobedience in a unit. And if we men had complained against Captain Rollins, we would have been disobeying, and that would have meant trouble.

"Now I know what you've heard—that the militia is just a poorly organized band of rabble-rousers anyway. There is some truth to that, I'll own, but for all his meanness, Captain Rollins was a good soldier and trained us well. Shoot, if we had more of what we needed, and proper supplies, we might really have a shot at defending our homes, if the chance comes our way.

"Anyway. One day, about a twelvemonth back, Captain Rollins stumbled into the camp, blind drunk, with a … ahem … young lady on his arm. Now, that business is strictly prohibited. General Washington will have your commission for that kind of nonsense. Militia camps are—I'll remind you, Miss Summerton—dangerous and inappropriate places for ladies, and Rollins knew that. Not to mention it's a plain rule, and rules apply to the captain as well.

"So that evening James McLean was on watch when Rollins and his lady friend showed up. Now James, he's a quiet sort, but he is solid goodness down to his core, and that's no lie, Anne. When he saw the captain and his girl, he just flatly refused to let him into the camp. Yes, just like that. He said, 'No, sir, Captain Rollins, you can't bring that lady in here.'

"Well, you can imagine that Rollins was fit to be tied. Angry and squawking like a hen, he starts to pistol-whipping poor James about the head, and James was brave—took the blows like a good lad. The commotion caused quite a stir among the camp, and soon enough most of the boys were up, peeking out of their tents, skulking about listening to the ruckus. Douglas himself woke up and was furious to see his son being beat down by the captain. So he picked up the closest thing to his hand—happened to be quite a large rock, Anne—and smashed it on the back of Rollins's head. Lucky he didn't kill him.

"Rollins keeled over to the ground, the girl ran off, and Douglas was beside himself with anger and worry about his boy."

I was growing impatient with his wandering narrative. "You are curiously missing from the story thus far, Captain Blake. I believed you told me you held a starring role."

"I'm about to tell you my role in the story, Anne! Be patient."

"Very well, then. Get to it."

"Well, of course the noise woke me up as well. I was kind of promoted to a second—just meant that I was able to take on more responsibility than some of the other boys. Just meant that Rollins liked me, really. So I was asleep by the captain's tent when the fight started and was at the scene directly when Douglas showed up with his rock. Seeing that Rollins was out cold, I set about cleaning up James's face and seeing to his wounds. He was cut up about his face but was not too bad off. I sent him back to his bed and summoned Billy to take his place on watch. Then Douglas and I dragged Rollins back to his bed, giving him a few solid punches about his face in the process. I cleaned up the camp and sent everybody to bed, but not before lecturing all the boys to follow my lead when Rollins woke up.

"Next morning, the captain had himself one heck of a headache between the whiskey and the blows he took. I never take whiskey myself, and that's why. He roared at me from his tent, asking what in the Almighty's name happened to his head.

"I told him, 'Sir, you were firmly in your cups last night, and two boys from the village brought you home, saying you'd been in a big fight in the alehouse.

"You see, Rollins had been so drunk he had no memory of what actually happened, and everybody in camp liked James so much, they all followed my story. As far as James's cuts, we just told the captain that he got into a scuffle with his brothers. Rollins never could tell the McLean boys apart anyway.

"That night Douglas came to me in the woods, all emotion. Said I saved his life and his boy's life too. Truth be told, Rollins probably would have tried to send them all to jail or the like—I told you, he was a good soldier but a nasty gentleman. Anyway, Douglas swore to always protect me and back me—to pay the debt back, so to speak. I told him that wasn't necessary, but you know, Anne, he's a handy fellow to have around.

"We've been thick ever since, even after I was sent up to Nelson's group. But right after I left, old Rollins found a way to boot the McLeans out of the militia anyway, and I wasn't around to help anymore."

I stared at him, mouth agape, while he finished his story with a flourish—a suspiciously self-satisfied smirk etched on his face.

"You are telling me a falsehood, Jonas Blake," I said.

His tone was indignant. "I most certainly am not, Anne. You can ask Douglas yourself when we get back to camp." He turned away in a huff, muttering unintelligibly.

"Captain Rollins indeed," I grumbled to myself, despairing at the sight of the dawn breaking the tree line. It would be an exhausting day, to be sure.

When we reached the camp we were surprised to see almost everybody awake. Tom and Betsy were still abed, but we could hear the murmurs of the McLean men, grouped around the fire. As I drew nearer, I could see an extra man among them—tall and powerful, with a silver-streaked auburn ponytail. I heard Jonas's gasp. He clenched my arm and walked me swiftly to the fire. Douglas looked up from his mug of tea, grinning broadly at us both.

"Ah, Jonas, Miss Anne. So glad to see you back in camp."

Jonas was tense beside me. "Any word from Nelson's scouts?"

Douglas began to answer, but a strong Scottish brogue interrupted him. "We sent those boys back south, Mr. Blake. Do not fear them. Now, introduce me to your lady friend."

Jonas squeezed by hand. "Anne, meet Logan Campbell."

IN WHICH I STAND
MY GROUND

"Good morning, Mr. Campbell." I bobbed a gentle curtsey and placed my hand in his large and callused one. "I am Anne Summerton."

The auburn-haired man squeezed my hand—his penetrating gaze roaming over my face, sizing me up.

Well, at least now I could look at him closely of my own accord, not trying to sneak furtive glances across a crowded, open-air pagan festival. I squared my shoulders and met his stare, hoping my boldness concealed my quavering insides. Logan was indeed powerfully built, but his manners were refined, gentlemanly—he couldn't have become king of his county without them. His skin was weathered from years in the field—drawn taut over high cheekbones—and his eyes were a cold, clear green. It was plain he was an intelligent, calculating man, and I was currently his field of inquiry.

He nodded sharply at me. "Miss Summerton, have a seat and a mug of tea while we discuss your problem."

Jonas lowered me onto the nearest tree stump gingerly, minding my sore limbs.

Douglas noticed the movement and glanced sharply at Jonas. "And what is ailing Miss Anne this fine morning, Jonas?"

Jonas scowled at his friend. "We had some uncomfortable hiding last night."

Douglas nodded. "Aye, and you just *had* to take her on your flight, did you?"

The dark scowl on Jonas's features became positively stormy. "I wasn't going to leave her there with all of those—" he stopped abruptly, glancing at Logan.

Douglas grinned wickedly.

"Anne is perfectly well," Jonas finished curtly, dropping on the ground next to me.

"Abbingdon," I murmured faintly, to remind the men why we were gathered.

However, Logan Campbell was already bobbing his head. "Yes," he said. "It is quite a puzzle, Miss Summerton. How this Mr. Norrington has managed to take advantage of the whole county irritates me in the extreme."

I glanced at Jonas, wondering if he, too, caught the irony in Logan's statement. The scarcely visible smirk at the corner of his mouth told me he did. He and Douglas had chosen Mr. Campbell well. Very well.

"What do you think can be done, sir?" I asked.

He seemed to be in a trance—staring at the fire, rubbing his long fingers across his russet stubble, occasionally muttering to himself. Douglas nodded slightly; he alone seemed relaxed, while Jonas and I waited, seemingly at the end of our rope.

Logan leaned back and breathed deeply. "Well," he finally said, "it would seem best to ride up to Abbingdon with some boys and speak to Mr. Norrington. Now, you understand, miss, that an all-out fight wouldn't be the wisest course of action just yet." He swung his eyes over to Jonas shrewdly. "We certainly don't want the militia looking our way, do we?"

Jonas smiled coolly but said nothing.

"Give me twenty-four hours. I'll return tomorrow at daybreak with my men." Logan stood up.

As they made their way to their mounts, I watched them closely—the scene was an amazing study in personalities. Douglas, the jovial loyal friend, was nodding his oversized head in agreement, eager for a fight; Logan, the master, was waving his hands about in command, clearly in control; and finally Jonas, unlabeled, still a mystery to me, was meeting Logan's gaze directly and yet refusing to readily assent to his commands. I shook my head in wonder—what would eventually become of this crew and their strategy, only God could know.

After a lengthy conversation, Logan mounted his horse and rode toward the south. Douglas and Jonas strode back to the fire, talking in low tones and glancing at me.

Of course, I thought, *why include Anne on the important matters? She is, after all, the entire reason we are gathered here.*

Jonas reached my side, pulling me up by my elbow.

"Come, Anne," he said. "You should lie down to rest. You were awake most of the night."

I scowled at Douglas over my shoulder, fully aware that something was in the works, but allowed Jonas to lead me to my tent. He was just about to deposit me through the flap when I stopped in my tracks and faced him.

"I know you three were discussing me. Tell me what that was all about."

Jonas sighed and rubbed his temples. It dawned on me that he, too, had been awake through the night and was as tired and worn as I.

"Come, Jonas."

He sighed, turning his tired blue gaze on me. "No. Not now. I am too tired to battle with you. Go and lie down, and I'll come for you later."

I turned from him and bustled through my tent flap, flopping down on my bedroll. Surprisingly, neither my frustration at the men nor Betsy's gentle snoring were able to keep sleep away for long.

I was rudely awakened by Betsy's tortured squeal. "Anne! Oh, Anne!"

Bolting upright, I glanced around me, halfway expecting our tent to be filled with wayward soldiers. A quick survey of our area showed that we were safely alone. Betsy was neither bleeding nor broken, as far as my eye could see. It was not storming, cold, or burning inside our tent. I felt no shooting pain in my body, save for sore limbs, and I saw no blood or corpses laid out on our floor. And yet, here was my sister, her face twisted in shock, her voice emitting in high-pitched yelps.

"Anne! My goodness, Anne!"

I rubbed my eyes quickly and squinted at her. "Bets, what *is* it?" I groaned in frustration. "What on earth is the matter?"

She lifted a shaking hand and gestured to my person. "Your dress," she shrieked, "it's *ruined!*"

True enough, a glance at my body proved her tale. The green fabric was torn in several places. What wasn't torn was caked in mud. The bodice was separated from the overskirt—somehow the stomacher had detached itself. I was no expert seamstress, though I was easily able to mend torn clothes. This, however, was beyond either of our abilities.

"Yes, I know, Bets. But perhaps you could have waited until I was awake to point it out?"

"What happened?"

"I fled the soldiers with Jonas. How did you fare with James and Tom? Did they keep you safe?"

She nodded, her violet eyes bobbing along with her blonde curls. "Oh, yes. That James is a smart lad, Anne. He got Tom and me away safely enough. We were even able to stay a while longer at the party. It is a great shame that you had to miss the end."

Too tired and frustrated to even think of that reality, I nodded stiffly and disrobed, casting aside my ruined dress. There was naught to do but wear the other new one from Douglas and hope that all-night slumbers in the bushes were at their end. As I was putting it on and Betsy was lacing the back, we heard an *ahem* from the tent flap.

"Who is it?" I called, as if Betsy and I—the only two ladies in the camp—would allow anybody into our tent while dressing.

"Can I speak to you, Anne?" It was Jonas, his voice kind and almost contrite.

So now we hear it, I thought.

"Just a moment, Jonas." I called, patiently enduring Betsy's pulling and yanking at my hair and dress until I was fit to be seen. I glanced down at my dress, feeling pretty and quite presentable. Glancing up at Betsy, I smiled.

"You look terrible," she whispered.

I was shocked. Surely that couldn't be so. "*What? Why?*" I smoothed the folds of my skirt and pouted. "It's lovely."

"It's not the dress, Anne." She pinched at my cheeks and pulled at my eyelids. "You look deathly tired. Your face is drawn, and you have giant pockets under your eyes. You need a good night's rest in a nice, soft bed."

I groaned. "I don't see that coming for many a day, Betsy."

Taking my worn shawl from the tent post, I flounced out of the flaps to find Jonas waiting patiently, his face strained. When he saw me he gazed quickly over my face and pursed his lips.

"You look tired, Anne," he said.

Well, that was just enough! "Goodness sakes!" I said, walking quickly away from him toward I didn't know where. "I am *not* tired. I do not *look* tired. I am *not* weak. I am *not* sick or in pain. I am *completely* well and able to handle this!" My voice was growing higher in pitch with each proclamation—my legs striding dangerously toward the forest's edge where I would surely get lost once again.

I heard Jonas fast at my heels; he quickly grasped my elbow and pulled me to a stop, wheeling me about to face him. My chest was heaving in anger and exertion—the worst part about my outburst being that none of those firm assertions were actually true. My sister was right—I sorely needed rest in a nice bed and a respite from all of this strain.

Jonas sensed this. He said nothing—just allowed me to calm down and offered me his arm. "Let's walk," he said.

We strolled a piece away from the camp. It was early afternoon—I slept about five hours before Betsy's alarm at the state of my frock interrupted my nap. Although it was mid-summer, our proximity to both the river and the ocean brought a comfortable breeze to the air. It was lush and green near the edge of the forest and altogether relaxing, as long as I could keep my troublesome thoughts at bay. I tried to do so for the first silent fifteen minutes of our walk, and then I could bear it no longer.

"Jonas, no more silence. What is your plan?"

Jonas sighed, briefly taking my hand and squeezing it. "We were thinking it best if you and Betsy stayed away from the, er, confrontation back in Abbingdon, just a day's ride from here. That way you and Betsy would stay safe for certain." His words came out in a teeming rush, as if he were trying to impede my interruption. "I know it's several days' ride from Abbingdon to the McLean place, but it is the safest place to stow you during the fight."

At a glance this plan seemed very sensible. There would be an altercation, surely. It would possibly—probably—erupt into violence. Betsy and I could quite easily get caught in the results of that fight—could get hurt or even accidentally killed, as poor Nate had. The plan made complete and total sense.

Except it didn't.

This was, from the start, my own fight. I'd have fought it with my own hands if I were a man, in possession of the power and sway that a man of standing carried. The farm was the result of my own toil and lost youth. The vacuum created by Mother's death and Father's illness was filled entirely by me. I swallowed my own pride and hurt so we could beg for Jonas to assist us. I had been kidnapped, beaten, dragged through the muck, and stashed under bushes. I did not intend to stay home from my own party.

I sized up Jonas's face before digging in my heels. He was regarding me warily, yet I sensed an air of humor about him. More irritated than amused, I narrowed my eyes at him to show that I did not fear him. He merely returned my stare with equal obstinacy, his mouth lifting slightly at the corner.

Finally he sighed. "Well, out with it, Anne. I know you've a strong opinion on the matter."

I crossed my arms and lifted my chin haughtily. "I am *not* staying here. I'm coming with you."

Jonas nodded shortly, turning and starting back toward the camp. "Very well."

He began to walk slightly in front of me, not lending me his arm as he did before. I skipped a step so I could catch up with him, craning my neck to seize a glimpse of his reaction.

He was grinning from ear to ear.

That Jonas Blake was always one step ahead of me.

IN WHICH JONAS AND I
REACH AN ACCORD

Although Logan Campbell said he would return in twenty-four hours, time seemed to stretch far beyond a single day. The remainder of that day was a blur of resting, pacing, trying to eat, and finally collapsing on my bedroll for a few hours of troubled sleep.

Just before nightfall, Douglas, James, Betsy, Tom, Jonas, and I sat around the fire—each lost in our own thoughts. The horses were packed for our dawn departure. When the silence became too deafening, Tom and I took to wondering what would await us when we reached our home.

"Have you even thought about Father?" I asked him quietly, not wishing for Betsy to overhear. However, evidently weary of the silence herself, she was in close conversation with James McLean across the fire. I wasn't much concerned.

The firelight played on Tom's pained features. "Of *course*, but what can be done about it now? It's two days' ride to Abbingdon at least—there's not a thing we can do for him between now and then, Anne."

I nodded and leaned my head against his shoulder, but I couldn't stay still for very long. I lifted my head. "But Tom, suppose he..."

"Hush, Anne."

It was a supposition I was reluctant to utter as well.

Another long silence stretched between us.

At length Tom shifted next to me and spoke again. "Anne, promise me you'll stay at the house with Betsy. No running off and getting into trouble."

"Why, Thomas!" I huffed. "I would never—"

"Yes," Tom interrupted, "you *would*. *You*, sister, will be hard pressed to sit aside and let the rest of us handle this problem."

Recalling my earlier conversation with Jonas, I saw some truth to Tom's words. Unwilling to admit that, however, I held my tongue.

"Well?" he said.

I refused to meet his eyes. "Well, what, Thomas?"

He plucked my chin in his hand and scowled at me.

"Do you promise to keep your nose clean?"

I delayed as long as possible before answering, but he was right, and I was loath to deny my brother anything he wanted. "Oh, very well," I said. "I'll do my best."

Tom released my chin and leaned back against his tree stump, grinning. "Ah, you're a good girl, Anne. So compliant."

I chuckled to myself over that for a few minutes before falling asleep by the fire.

The dawn light was just barely shimmering into the camp when we heard hoof beats approaching from the south. I opened my eyes slowly, trying to gain my bearings. Jonas and Douglas were up, scanning the horizon and watching for the approaching horsemen. Tom held my arm protectively; across the extinguished fire James was likewise shielding Betsy. Our group waited in tense silence as the sound grew nearer.

Suddenly, the first riders appeared at the far end of our clearing. It was Logan Campbell, followed by at least twenty men. I gathered there were at least that many still following. I breathed a sigh of relief. Our help had come, he was here, and we were ready to ride home.

The ride home was far shorter than our voyage south. Experienced horsemen who knew the country apparently made a great deal of difference.

Jonas and Douglas rode in the front, as Jonas was most likely to know the best way to Abbingdon. Betsy and I followed them, flanked by Tom and James. Campbell and his men rode a slight distance behind us. The journey was mostly silent—the stillness at times broken by a shared comment here and there. Laughter was scarce, and tension was high. Occasionally, I would hear Jonas and Douglas whisper to one another; whatever their topic was, they were not sharing it with Betsy and me. The lack of entertainment became stifling. By the end of the first day, I was drifting to sleep in my saddle.

"Easy, Anne." Tom nudged me awake after the second time I nearly fell off of my mount.

"Try to stay awake, Anne. We need you to be alert," Jonas called over his shoulder.

I scowled at his back.

"I can't help it," I said to Tom. "It is so still and quiet. Not nearly diverting enough to keep me awake."

Tom just grinned.

"How much longer until we can stop and rest?" I called to nobody in particular, although I knew Jonas was listening.

"Another hour, Anne. You can do it," he said.

My mood was growing sour with this ride.

True to his promise, though, Jonas called a halt less than an hour later. Our small group dismounted and hobbled the horses. Jonas rode a distance back to the Campbell men to tell them our plans to rest for the night.

I turned to Douglas. "Why don't the Campbell men camp with us? Wouldn't that be safer?"

Douglas glanced around furtively, his eyes narrowing to slits. "Between you and me, Miss Anne," he whispered, "I'm not rightly sure Mr. Jonas trusts those men around you and your bonnie sister."

"I see."

"Twenty men is a mighty big mob to be gathered around two pretty lasses, if you catch my meaning, Miss Anne."

I caught it readily enough and was thankful for Jonas's insight. Likely I would sleep better knowing the Campbell men weren't close enough to creep upon Betsy and me in the night. "Will we be using our tents tonight, Douglas?" I asked, realizing that he held very little authority in the matter.

He smiled and shrugged. "We'll ask Mr. Jonas when he returns, miss."

I nodded and limped toward the edge of the clearing, looking about for a wide-open space to lie down and rest before meal preparations began. It really was a lovely little meadow—the sort that littered the Virginia countryside and inspired the settlers to stay long ago. A semicircle of trees surrounded a lush green field, the grass bright and irresistibly soft. In my mind's eye, I pictured a quaint, white farmhouse there with a *small* garden—as much as I loved my father's land, the sheer amount of the planting acres was daunting—and room for children to run around. My small fantasy was going to turn wayward any moment, so I tried to focus my thoughts on our present fears.

"Anne? What are you doing?"

I snapped my head about and saw Jonas a few paces behind me, his face tense. In fact, his entire body was stiff with anxiety. The poor man had had little chance to rest since I stumbled into his camp days ago.

"I'm perfectly well, Jonas, just looking for a quiet place to lie down before we eat. I am spent."

The tension released from Jonas's shoulders; they seemed to lose their rigidity before my eyes.

I smiled, amused. "Why don't *you* try resting as well?"

"I believe I will."

Jonas crumpled before me, his knees buckling beneath him as he fell to the ground. I rushed over to him, relieved to see that he had only taken my suggestion very seriously. He stretched out on the soft grass, limbs relaxed, face still. I stretched out next to him several inches away and watched the clouds move for a time. It was the most peaceful I'd felt in days, and I surmised Jonas felt the same way.

"Anne," he began some time later, his voice alert and crisp.

"Yes?" My own voice was lazy and drowsy, as if I'd been pulled from a dream.

"This has been a pleasant rest, hasn't it?"

"Mmm-hmm."

We were quiet for a few moments, before Jonas spoke again.

"It seems I can only rest easy when I know you are safe."

His words shocked me out of my reverie. I knew not what to say next, so I held my tongue and continued to stare at the darkening sky.

He said nothing more, and my emotions grew muddled. It would be far simpler if he did *not* care … yet did he care really, or was he just being protective? I couldn't allow myself to entertain such thoughts again—they were wholly counter-productive to our mission and must be stopped. By some alien strength I sat up.

"It must be time to eat soon. We should go back to the fire." I stood, brushing the grass off of my ridiculously out-of-place dress.

Jonas stood as well, walking behind me while pulling grass blades out of my laces and skirts. "Your poor green frock was ruined, all because of me," he said. "I will tell Douglas to give you a new one from his stash."

He smiled at me, and I bit my lip, trying to keep my feelings at bay.

"Yes, um, that would be lovely," I stammered, taking a step away from him.

Jonas opened his mouth, hesitated, and then opened it again. "Anne"—his voice was low, all seriousness— "tomorrow Douglas and I will split off from the group with the Campbells. James and Tom will see you safely to your house and then join us in town."

"And the rest of the McLeans?"

"They will meet us in Abbingdon."

I nodded, fear beginning to creep over me. It's as if I had forgotten that tomorrow—*tomorrow*—we would be home and the fighting would begin.

Jonas took my hand in his. "I know that I haven't treated you with much kindness these recent days. God knows I've been stubborn in forgiving you and your family for what happened between us."

"Jonas, please!" I cried, pulling my hand away. My emotions railed between eagerness and panic. I desperately wanted to hear him out, but I also feared the power his words might have over me. "There's no call to bring that up right now. It was a long time ago."

"Yes, it was." He nodded. "And for my part in it, I'm quite sorry, Anne. Truly."

I nodded, relieved that he said nothing further. "Me as well. I don't know what else I can say. I regret it, Jonas."

He stared at the ground a moment, while I watched the wind ruffle his brown hair. Deep breaths could only conceal my anxiety for so long. I was thankful his gaze was not resting on me.

At length he brought his eyes to mine, plucking my hand from my side. "Please, Anne, please, keep yourself and Betsy safe tomorrow. Promise me?"

For a moment I wished to protest. Why were all the men assuming I was reckless and bent on danger? The assault on my character was difficult to bear. I opened my lips to object but thought better of it. He did appear so earnestly concerned for me, and I didn't wish to upset our recently achieved peace. I nodded.

Jonas dropped my hand, guiding me through the dusk back to the fire.

I slept restlessly that night. Jonas had prohibited the use of our tents, so once again we spread out on our bedrolls near the fire, under the stars. Betsy and I were sandwiched between Tom and James, both of whom quickly fell asleep. Betsy and I were not so lucky. For my part, my mind was consumed with fears for the coming days, and I was consequently uninterested in sleep. Whatever was plaguing Betsy, she was tossing on the uncomfortable ground to my right.

"Anne?"

"Yes, Bets?"

"Supposing all of this works out and Norrington leaves us alone and we keep our farm, but then Father dies. What will happen then?"

Betsy's query was one I had considered myself. Even if this confrontation worked out in our favor, we would end up in the same dilemma—dirt-poor with no men to run the farm and no farmhands to tend the fields. And what of the war itself? How much damage would it wreak havoc on our village? A dozen Jonas Blakes couldn't stem that tide.

I shrugged in the darkness. "I don't know, Betsy."

"It's a shame that some of the McLean boys can't be our farmhands," she said. "James told me he has two brothers. They're plenty big enough to be farmhands."

I grinned in the darkness, pinching her cheek. "Why, Betsy!" I said. "I believe you're sweet on James McLean!"

"Anne!" she shrieked, struggling to keep her voice low. After all, the object of our discussion was lying just on the other side of her. "Don't even say so. It ain't proper."

"Betsy, in these times, some proper things must be cast aside."

"I s'pose you're right."

"Of course I am."

The conversation stalled for a time.

I was almost asleep when she had the last word. "I ain't sweet on him," she muttered.

I snickered to myself before drifting off to sleep.

The next morning dawned hot and humid. The thought of the long ride ahead made me wish I could sleep a little longer. As I opened my eyes and rolled to my side, I groaned at the sight of my horse hobbled nearby. "I do not wish to sit on your back all day," I muttered.

"I was thinking you'd take the horse," Tom answered from his bedroll, just a few inches away.

I chuckled loudly, my mood already improved, diverted by Tom's good humor.

Our party roused and assembled quickly to ride for Abbingdon. My standard emotion of the age—fear—was blessedly smothered that morning by an eagerness to get home to Father and see how he fared. A similar, fervent excitement spread throughout the camp. The men all seemed ready to go, keen for action.

We rode for several hours before pausing for a quick midday meal. After beginning again, it was only a matter of hours before the countryside turned familiar. Unwelcome nerves clenched my stomach; the time for action drew nigh.

Please, God, I prayed, *make this right.*

The men in front stopped, turning their horses about to face us.

"Ladies," Jonas said, "this is where we leave you. Tom, you know the way from here?"

Tom nodded. "Sure thing, Jonas."

Jonas smiled. "Very well. James, you help Tom keep the ladies safe, then ride with Tom into the village. Stay sharp, mind you. There's no telling what you'll find when you reach us."

James nodded, sneaking a glance at Betsy and smiling.

Douglas and Jonas rode back toward the Campbell party. I turned on my mount to watch them go, wondering what our world would be like when I saw them again. James, Betsy, and Tom trotted forward, but I remained to watch the men's retreating backs. I willed Jonas to turn and bid me farewell, hurt at his abrupt departure. Alas, he did not obey, but continued steadfastly forward. I sighed and turned to face the journey home.

Not two moments later, I heard hoof beats pounding behind me. My body tensed as I drew reign and wheeled about. I sighed in relief at the sight of Jonas. "Don't do that to me, Jonas Blake! Call out in warning or something! You frightened me so!"

Jonas grinned and shook his head. "You never make it easy on a man, you know that, Anne? Not ever."

I was still catching my breath as he drew his horse closer. "Make what easy?"

Jonas didn't answer. He just closed the distance between us, pulled me to him, and kissed me soundly on the lips. A jolt of electricity rushed through me, rendering me quite senseless. My horse angled beneath me, and truth told, my entire world unsettled. I rested one hand on Jonas's shoulder and one on my saddle to keep myself steady—it wouldn't do to fall off my horse at this particular moment. Jonas, likewise, had one hand on his own horse and the other cradling my head, his fingers laced through my hair. My mind tried to determine why exactly he was kissing me; other parts of me didn't rightly care *what* his reasons were.

It was over too quickly. Jonas pulled away, smiling. "Keep your promise, Anne!" With that farewell, he galloped away to join his men.

I sighed. My stomach was roiling, both from the kiss and from the anxiety of the coming day. Before I had even a second to process what had just happened, Jonas was out of sight.

IN WHICH WE LOSE
SOMETHING PRECIOUS

The remainder of the ride to our farm passed quickly. Early on, after Jonas's departure, the mood was light and jovial—somehow the gravity of our mission was temporarily forgotten—and James, Tom, Betsy, and I enjoyed lively conversation and laughter. However, as we drew within miles of our home, the dark thoughts returned, and we Summertons, for our part, regained our seriousness.

I half expected to see Will Norrington established in our home, our father dead and buried, and the sign at the post changed to "Norrington Farm." Fortunately, as the path to our home came into view, it was plain that those fears were not a reality—yet.

We had been away little more than a fortnight, but the house looked lonely for our short absence. I recalled I was in the potato fields planting when events unfolded and ridiculously found myself praying that rain had fallen while we were away. We drew rein at the door, leaping from our mounts; James gladly stabled them for us so we could rush inside to see our father.

Mary Hudgins sat sewing by the kitchen fire as we burst into the house, dusty and dirty from our long travels. She looked up in surprise. "Betsy! Tom! Anne! Hello!" Mary was smiling—not at all tired, drawn, or saddened, but smiling.

I nearly collapsed on the floor in a relieved heap.

"Mary," Tom moved as swiftly as he could across the floor, kneeling at her feet. "How is Father?"

Mary cocked her head, her pretty smile still static on her face. "Well, he's fine, Tom. Not much improved since you went away, but not worse either."

Tom turned and looked at us, and Betsy and I did indeed burst into happy tears. We put our arms around each other and walked in tandem up the stairs to see Father.

By the time darkness fell, we'd been home scarcely two hours and had not strayed from Father's bedside. If he was asleep, we simply sat near him, smiling through our grateful tears. And when he roused, we told him of our adventure: the quest for Jonas, meeting the McLean family, the pagan barn dance, and the feisty Logan Campbell. He smiled when he could. Despite Mary's assertions that Father had not grown any worse in his illness, it was plain to me that he was weakening, and fast.

Initially, we were all so happy to be back and near him that I gave nary a thought to Jonas or the conflict possibly taking place in town. But my complacency didn't last. Tom and James soon left to join the others, and we'd heard nothing since then. As pleasant as home felt, especially near Father, I was getting itchy feet not knowing what was taking place.

"Blast those boys," I muttered to myself—wishing to high heaven they hadn't been right about me. Well, I would show them. I *would* sit in our home—all domestic-like, reading or sewing or tending to Father—and not give two whits about the boys and their fighting.

But first I was in desperate need of a bath. I fetched my satchel to remove my dirty petticoats and stockings and found there another new dress—a beautiful cream-colored calico with a high neck and elbow-length, ruffled sleeves. Somehow, Jonas must have ferreted it from Douglas's ready supply and placed it in my bag. I smiled in spite of myself, allowing a moment to remember his kiss before busying myself otherwise.

The bath was divine. Scrubbing the days of dirt and dust away was like removing another skin. I dare not recall the last time I had bathed—it was too shocking to reflect upon. I rolled my wet hair and donned my new frock, feeling instantly more like myself.

I entered the parlor, long vacated by our guest, Mary, and found Betsy by the fire, wringing her hands.

"Anne," she said, "something's wrong with Father."

I sat down on the sofa and sighed. "Yes, Betsy. He's very ill. Worse than Mary let on, I believe."

Betsy rushed to my side and squeezed my arm. "No, Anne, I mean something's gone wrong *now*. Just since you've gone to the bath. You must go and see him."

My poor sister, who had not yet bathed to improve *her* mood, was anxious, tired, and dirty. It was my default reaction to chide her for her fretting, but not today. Instead, I patted her hand. "Betsy," I said, "go on and have a bath. I'll go tend to Father for a while. He is probably just overtired from our homecoming."

She sighed in plain relief, the exhaustion showing on her features. "Yes, I'm sure you're right, Anne. I will go and bathe."

As Betsy slumped away into the bathing room, I trudged up the stairs to see Father. I entered his room, immediately recognizing that something in this place was wrong. To own the truth, it smelled of death.

Realizing what I was facing, I rushed to Father's side and picked up his hand, which, thankfully, was still warm.

"Father, Father! It's Anne. Please wake and tell me how I can help you."

His eyelids fluttered; his head moved from side to side on his damp pillow. "Anne? Anne..."

I squeezed his limp hand. "Yes, I'm here."

His words came slowly, laboriously. "I've been waiting for you."

"For me? Well... here I am. I'll stay here all night. As long as you need me."

So great had been our happiness upon returning home, we had gladly gathered around Father and enjoyed our reunion. Our concern for his illness had been buried beneath relief from simply seeing him again. But now I looked at Father—really looked at him—and saw the vast differences in his features. His skin had turned sallow and loose, his gaunt cheeks seemingly unable to hold it smooth. His breath entered and exited his lungs with great pain and hesitation. And his eyes, the deep gray eyes that Tom and I had inherited, were glassy and unfocused.

The situation was grave. As ill as he'd been for many months now, I had never seen him like this. A creeping sadness overtook me as I realized I would lose him, and soon. I was alone with a dying man. Tom—gone. Jonas—gone. Betsy, who didn't need to be in there anyway—safely tucked away in the bath. It was just me, Father, whatever angels were waiting to bear him hence, and God.

"Thank you … "

"For what, Father?"

"Fetching Jonas. He will help you." His every word was rasping, hoarse—spoken with a desperate amount of effort on his part.

Tears began to well up in my eyes. I squeezed Father's hand until I thought it would break clean off. "I hope he will, Father."

"Anne … "

"Yes? I'm here."

"I'm sorry … to you both. Should have let you and Jonas marry."

"Father, no! You were right. I was too young. I am still too young."

My father's thin shoulders imitated a nonchalant shrug. He was still trying to be strong and didactic, as in days of old. "Maybe … but he's a good man."

"He is indeed, Father."

He sputtered and coughed. I grasped his shoulders, trying to help steady him. He fell back on his pillow, his breathing labored, barely able to say his next sentence.

"You could still marry him."

Shock and grief overwhelmed me—my shoulders slumped. The thought of marrying Jonas was indeed delightful but was not to be entertained at Father's bedside. I shook my head. "I don't *care* about that now, Father. I just want you to be well."

"I'm not going to get well, Anne."

Tears spilled over and down my face. I let go of Father's hands just quickly enough to brush them away from my cheeks. This was indeed too much to bear—I had so hoped we could save the farm *for* Father. I had not considered we would save it without him.

"Anne, if you love him you have my blessing."

I collapsed on the bed next to him, my tears drenching the coverlet. My whole body rejected what was happening—I was shaking in violent spasms, my voice choking, unstoppable tears flooding out. I can't say how long I lay next to Father crying; all I can say is that when my tears were spent and emotion drained, he was gone.

I stared at Father longingly. To be truly alone in the world without a mother or father—what on earth was God thinking? How could I possibly go on without Father? Even during his illness, as I shouldered the farm alone, I still had a father. He was always there, even if *there* was the upstairs bedroom. And now he was truly gone.

In my despair God's sweet Spirit reminded me that I would never be fatherless. I cried out to the presence that had been so faithful these past weeks—that he bid me strength in this, the darkest of hours.

I trudged downstairs, finding Betsy clean and smiling at the table. The bath had improved her mood as it had mine. The tea things lay fresh and neat before her on the table.

"And how does he fare?" she asked.

It's ill of me to think it, but I nearly lied to her and told her he was sleeping and hoped that Tom would come home and discover Father's lifeless body. The lie would strengthen me; whereas telling Betsy would sap what little power I had left in me. But the presence protested. Surely our Father in heaven could supply Betsy's needs as he had mine.

I took Betsy's hands, squeezed them, and looked into her violet eyes. There was no need for further conversation. Betsy crumpled into my arms as we stumbled toward the couch, comforting each other and receiving comfort from God.

By the time we had exhausted our grief, night had fallen, and an eerie calm floated throughout our land. The absence of news from the men in town was beginning to wear on me, but that anxiety was buried beneath our new loss.

Betsy fell asleep just after nightfall. I stoked the fire and paced the parlor, drinking cold tea and hard biscuits—waiting. Waiting for something. Something must be happening.

At length I heard hoof beats in the lane. I rushed to the kitchen door, hurrying out onto the porch and nearly running plumb into Tom. At the sight of my favorite person, the tears began anew. One look at my face, and he understood. He held me with his arm as we leaned against the porch railing in the dark.

After another interlude of weeping, Tom asked, "Did he say anything?"

I sniffled and wiped my face with my handkerchief. "Yes. Actually, he told me to go on and marry Jonas if I wished."

Tom wheeled back, eyes wide. "And do you wish?"

Sighing, I leaned once more into his shoulder. "I can't think about that now, Thomas."

Tom stiffened as he pulled away from me. "That's true, Anne, you can't. You derailed me with your news, and now it's time to tell you mine. And, sister, we will need all of your strength of spirit to get out of this one."

"Tom! No! What is it? Tell me. Is Jonas well?"

He nodded quickly, rubbing his hand along the back of his neck. "Well enough, Anne. Jonas and Douglas were out in the woods, waiting for the rest of the McLeans. About dusk we all rode into town together to see Norrington."

"That late? We'd been here for hours by then!"

"True, and it was our undoing. While we were waiting on the McLeans, Logan tells us he'll ride ahead. 'See the lay of the town,' he says. Well, when we met up and rode into town, turns out that they were all in formation against us—ready for a fight."

"All?"

Tom nodded. "All, Anne. Campbell and his men joined with Norrington."

The strength God had lent me seeped straight out of me in that moment. I felt like a small twig about to snap. I couldn't bear one more burden—my yoke was heavy enough. In my weakness, however, I found anger, and the rage filled me with a new heat and power. "That turncoat! That redheaded rascal! That... that *rakehell scoundrel!*"

"He's all that and a crafty fox besides. Been planning this from the beginning, he has. Had all of his men assembled with Norrington's, ready to take our men down in an instant."

"That... that!" I could think of no more names to call him from my ladylike lexicon. I could only sputter in anger. "Wait, Tom. How did you know he'd been planning this?"

"That's the worst of it, Annie," he said, squeezing my shoulder. "He's led Nelson's militia back up here—about fifty men with a nasty leader. They took Jonas and all the McLean boys prisoner, calling them all deserters."

I recalled Logan Campbell's words that brisk dawn a few days ago. "Don't you be worrying about the militia, Mr. Blake. We sent those boys back south." Send them south, he did—south to get their leader and meet him in Abbingdon to take Jonas.

Despite my fury and alarm, the presence filled me again. It didn't feed on my anger; rather it transformed it into something powerful. I recalled the Scripture instilled by my many Sundays at church from the book of Isaiah: "A bruised reed shall he not break, and the smoking flax shall he not quench: he shall bring forth judgment unto truth."

Briskly, I stood straight and wiped my eyes a last time. "Thomas," I said, "go on inside. Tend to Betsy. Take a bath. See to having someone arrange a service for Father."

Tom eyed me carefully, attempting to determine my mood. "What are you doing, Anne?"

"Taking care of this predicament," I said. "Now, where did you say the militia was holding the men?"

IN WHICH I RUIN
ANOTHER FROCK

A storm had risen, and the rain whipped my face as I rode through the darkness to the north side of the village. Riding straight through town—and through Campbell's small army—to the grove on the other side was not advisable. Instead, I cut across the country and circled around, approaching the grove from the north.

The grove was a popular spot for picnics, church meetings, and shady walks in the happier days of Abbingdon. It was a small clearing encircled by massive oak trees, ancient and tall and imposing; the surrounding forest was clear enough for an afternoon stroll or a game of hide and seek. I could well understand why the militia would establish his camp there—ample room for his tents and abundant trees for tying up prisoners.

I slowed to a walk as soon as I heard the voices of the soldiers. Tying my horse to a tree a fair distance away, I crept through the darkness toward the noise and the firelight, of which there was precious little due to the rain.

About fifty yards away, I could see a small cluster of tents, at least ten in number. Each tent held at least two soldiers, maybe four. My stomach lurched at the sight. Tom had said the unit was forty men strong—for what purpose? Forty men just to fetch Jonas and take him back to North Carolina? If such a force was required, I had far underestimated his abilities.

I brushed wet hair from my face and crept closer. Halfway between the tents and my position, I could see an arc of trees; about seven of them sported prisoners.

Jonas.

It had to be him and Douglas and the rest of the boys, but I required a closer look. It was imperative that I not be seen. Fortunately, the rain was my ally; nobody would want to stand guard on a night such as this. As the militia wasn't here to mount an attack, security was at a minimum. I slowly crouched down and crawled along the tree line until I was a few feet away from the prisoners. I was drenched to the skin and soaked with mud.

Blast it! Yet another dress ruined!

I was as close as possible without exposing my hiding place. I paused and squatted, fretting about what to do next, when I heard a whisper from the tree bank.

"Jonas?"

"What is it, Douglas?"

"I believe I hear something scampering about in the bushes behind you, lad."

My breath caught. So Jonas was tied to the tree closest to me. *That,* to be sure, was quite fortuitous! Muttering a quick prayer for unearthly strength, I called out in a hoarse whisper, "Jonas!"

In the dark I saw his form flinch, trying to crane his head in my direction, but the tree blocked his vision. "Anne?"

"Yes, it's me."

Simultaneously, I heard Jonas mutter a low curse and Douglas snicker merrily.

"Ah, our bonnie lass has come to rescue us, my boy!"

"So it would seem," Jonas said. "Anne!" he called. "Are you alone?"

"Yes."

"Come around to me, very slowly and quietly. There's no guard watching, so you'll be safe."

I did as he bid me, pausing to lift my skirts out of the mud and to wipe the sticky hair from my forehead.

"Aw, Anne, stop fiddling with your petticoats and come over here! I am tied to this tree! This is not the time to be missish!"

"Don't be so fussy! I am rescuing you, after all!"

His arms were wrapped behind the tree, his wrists tied securely. I sidled up to the tree, pressed my head to his shoulder, and choked back a silent sob of relief.

He turned his head toward me, smiling. "Lovely to see you, Anne."

I heard Douglas from the tree next to Jonas. "Evening, Miss Anne! Fancy meeting you here!"

I lifted my head and nodded. "Douglas."

Jonas leaned his head toward me, as close as he could reach. "Anne Summerton, I don't know whether to kiss you or wring your stubborn neck! Correct me if I'm mistaken, but I do recall your promise to stay home."

Gesturing to his bonds, I retorted, "It doesn't look to me that you have either option, Jonas Blake, seeing as you are bound, and I am not." Standing up straight and squaring my hands on my hips, I snapped, "Shall I go home, then?"

Jonas narrowed his eyes, still poised between elation and exasperation. "I suppose you could untie me, as you've come all this way."

I stepped behind the tree and began to work the knot that bound his wrists. But the rope was thick, the knot tight, and the whole mess slippery from the rain. Jonas attempted to coach me from the other side of the tree.

"Don't rush now, Anne. Take it slowly. Just work at the ropes. Ouch! You pinched me! Be careful!"

"Stop badgering me! I can't concentrate!"

Douglas chuckled from his post. "That's a feisty one you've got there, Jonas."

Jonas snorted as I continued to pull at his ropes. I was making absolutely no progress and grew more frustrated with each passing minute.

"Where is Tom?" Jonas asked to distract me, I imagined.

"He's at home with Betsy. I told him to stay."

"That was well done, Anne. Thank you. And your father? How is his health?"

I sniffled and didn't answer, just pulled ferociously at Jonas's bonds.

"Anne?"

I dropped my hands from my work and walked around the tree to face him. His countenance was filled with compassion. I put my hands on his shoulders and collapsed against his chest, crying quietly, wishing like the dickens that his arms were unbound so he could hold me.

"I'm so sorry, dearest Anne," he whispered. "Were you with him when it happened, or was he already gone when you arrived today?"

"I was there." I snuffled into his jacket. "He said ..."

But a voice interrupted us from behind. "Well, this is a sweet reunion, indeed!"

Jonas cursed under his breath. "Turn about, Anne," he commanded, all traces of emotion gone.

I did as he said. Three men approached our alcove. In the darkness I could only discern that the first gentleman was very tall, but I could not distinguish his features.

"Private Blake," the newcomer drawled. Jonas was a captain, of course, but his support of the McLeans had resulted in a demotion. "Am I to assume that this is the lovely Anne Summerton?"

Behind me I heard a thump, an *oof!* from Jonas, and then his muttered, "Yes, sir, it is."

"We have done a great deal of riding on your behalf, Miss Summerton. You have caused quite a stir in this town and among these men, to be sure! I am intrigued to meet the girl that holds Private Blake's puppet strings."

Puppet strings, indeed! That was far from the truth, and I would plainly tell him so! I opened my mouth to protest, but Jonas nudged me.

"Don't answer him. Just smile and nod."

Smile and nod? I could easily employ a superior performance. I curtsied with all of the false homage I could muster and smiled my most brilliant smile. "As you please, sir," I gushed, "and with whom do I have the pleasure of speaking?"

The man threw his head back and laughed. It echoed loud and strong in the resplendent forest. "Why, didn't Jonas tell you, dear? I am Major Rollins, his old friend."

Major Rollins. No longer a captain. So he wasn't a fabrication after all. That was, indeed, regretful.

"Come, Miss Summerton. We will converse in my quarters."

I had no means of remonstration, for Major Rollins immediately had two guards at my sides, shoving me forcefully toward his tent.

"Don't hurt her, you blackguard!" Jonas said from his post.

The major only snickered but did not give Jonas the satisfaction of an answer.

As we walked my mind tried to recall the details Jonas had shared with me about the man who was Jonas's superior officer in his first militia appointment. *Hmmm. Unsavory and unwholesome came to mind. Those descriptions were not entirely helpful. A good soldier? Only helpful if he was on our side. Unlikely. This could be thorny.*

We were rapidly approaching Rollins's accommodation, and I needed to conjure a way out of this dilemma, somehow freeing Jonas in the process. I should have simply prayed for help—who knows what would have occurred had I first sought God. Instead, my mind catalogued all of the horrors that could befall my friends and family should this situation take a turn for the worse. My body tensed with anxiety as I set my muddy boots inside the major's tent.

And then God was faithful and handed me the answer, reminding me of what Jonas had said—that Rollins "couldn't abide by the English." Now that, to be sure, was a helpful piece of information.

It was with a newfound peace and confidence that I sauntered— almost saucily, if I may say—into the slovenly quarters inhabited by Major Rollins. It was warm, well lit, and thoroughly untidy. The light enabled me to glimpse the good soldier's countenance. The major was truthfully a handsome gentleman. Well shaped, high browed, and clear skinned, he was clean and manicured, with a sturdy dark brown ponytail and hazel eyes. I imagined he was quite popular with the caliber of ladies that frequented militia camps.

I was *not* the type of lady that frequented militia camps. That one instance was a necessary exception.

The major reclined fluidly in his chair, motioning his guards to their position outside the door. "Will you sit, Miss Summerton?"

"Why, thank you, sir. I don't mind if I do." I somehow *felt* elegant and powerful, wet and mud-covered as I was. I knew that God was about to "bring forth judgment unto truth," and I, for one, was thankful to be on the winning side. I cocked my head and stared complacently at him, even batting my eyes once or twice, to own the truth. And Rollins, prideful sort that he was, was taken in by my pretty attempts at flattery.

"Miss Summerton, I can't imagine why a lovely girl such as yourself would take up with a rake like Jonas Blake."

I leaned forward in a conspiratorial manner. "Major, surely you realize the value of Captain Blake as a soldier and a leader? Did you not notice the clan of McLeans that followed him up here to save our little village? Surely that type of quality could be useful in the state militia, if not the Continental Army itself?"

Rollins eyed me carefully, intrigued. "Really? A leader and a soldier, you say? I call him a deserter and so does Nelson. He sent me here personally to fetch Jonas. I was"—he paused and swung his handsome face my way, grinning— "*formally* with the Sussex militia but have recently been acquired by General Nelson. My first order from the general was to retrieve his Captain Blake at once."

I waved my hand dismissively. "But he's not needed with Nelson! I was *there* at Nelson's camp, Major. Jonas was looking after young men playing cards! He wasn't fighting or even training those men. Surely Nelson's outfit hasn't missed his skills in this past fortnight of thumb-twiddling, now has it?"

Rollins grunted and rolled his eyes. The good soldier was growing wary of my arguments, it seemed. The assumption that I would simply fall at his feet like other simpering girls was quickly disproved by my defense of Jonas. Now it was time to speak the plain truth.

"Major, please listen," I began, dropping my feminine pretenses and attempting to appeal to his better nature. "You have the wrong men imprisoned, don't you see that? Will Norrington and Logan Campbell should be bound to those trees outside! Jonas and the rest are trying to rid this town of villains. Now, I know that Logan Campbell led you up here to take Jonas back, but do you know what he's done? What Norrington has done? He holds widows at bayonet point until they sign their land over to him. Threatened old couples to give him their farms. Ruled this town with tyranny, just so he could become lord over Sussex County. He has even allowed innocent people to be killed to stay in power."

Rollins said nothing. The corner of his mouth twitched; otherwise, his face was an immobile mask.

"You know," I continued, "to take over land by force, just because you have the means and the power to do so . . . to set up a little feudal kingdom such as this . . . well, it's almost"—I paused— "*English*."

That word, that very word that had divided our new colonies into Patriots and Tories, that word that inspired both quaking fear and righteous indignation in the hearts of new Americans up and down the seaboard, that word accomplished my goal. Rollins's face contorted into a steely mask of anger.

I continued, hoping to ride my good fortune until its end. "It would be a tragedy for these soldiers to fight, even die, against the redcoats, only to have tyrants like Norrington and Campbell transform our new-found republic into a new-fangled version of the Mother Country. I, personally, would despair to see such a waste of this war."

And Rollins would as well, I could plainly see.

He leaned forward in his chair, his handsome face now enraged. "Miss Summerton, what do you propose I do?"

I smiled. "Well, you should let Jonas and his boys go, to start."

IN WHICH I
DISOBEY ORDERS

It was with no small amount of smugness that I strode out of the officer's tent with the fuming Major Rollins, who immediately ordered his guards to untie Jonas and the McLean men. My grin was triumphant as I threw my arms around the now free Jonas, well pleased that he could embrace me in return. His features showed signs of agitation as he pulled away from me and ran his fingers over my temples, searching my face for violence.

"Did he harm you?" He cast an angry glance in Rollins's direction.

"No, not at all," I responded.

"Blake, unhand that girl! We have work to do, my boy!" Rollins snapped.

Surprised, Jonas obeyed. Rollins began barking out orders, rousing the sleeping men, and making preparations for the coming day. I gathered it was still a few hours before dawn, but Rollins had plans in mind, and every moment was precious.

As the men dispersed, rapid hoof beats indicated a newcomer in the clearing. The soldiers quickly armed and prepared to shoot; however, the dim pre-dawn light indicated it was my brother, Tom. Those assembled breathed a collective sigh of relief as I launched myself into his embrace.

"What are you doing here, Tom?"

"I couldn't stay with Betsy any longer. Mary and her mother are sitting with her and, er, tending to Father."

"Father," I repeated softly, pressing my forehead to Tom's shoulder.

Jonas and the others left us for a few moments as the preparations for the fight resumed.

"Tom, are you going with Jonas?"

"Yes, ma'am. I'm not sitting out of this one."

"But Tom," I said, curious but not wishing to hurt his feelings, "you can't handle a musket."

Tom pulled away from me and jutted his chin out. "That's where you're wrong, sister. While you and Blake have been mooning about in the woods, Douglas here taught me to shoot one-handed."

"One-handed? Indeed! But how on earth will you reload?"

Tom's grin was sheepish. "That's the only problem, Annie. I can only shoot once."

I laughed heartily, bending at the waist and slapping my thigh. "Well, Tom, let's hope once is all that's required."

Major Rollins, who couldn't abide by folks being idle, interrupted our good humor. "Miss Summerton! Make yourself useful and help out with breakfast, my lass!"

"Duty calls." I chuckled, ambling away to the fire.

I must say I'd never expected to see myself sharing coffee and biscuits with militiamen, but it was not an unpleasant experience. Jonas, however, was so wary of the men's eyes on me he could barely relax enough to eat his own meal. After breakfast was finished, I made myself useful by taking James McLean with me to the nearby creek to do the washing.

"Miss Anne, did I hear Mr. Jonas say that your father passed last night?"

James was so kind I couldn't fault him for asking, even if the subject knocked me over with a fresh wave of grief. "Yes, he did, James."

He paused momentarily to help me lift a heavy pot filled with cold creek water. "And how does Miss Summerton fare?"

I smiled in spite of the cheerless topic. "She is tolerably well, James. Our close acquaintances are home with her. If this morning's ride is successful, you can all come to my house and pay your respects."

James ducked his head away from me. "Yes, I would like that, Miss Anne."

We finished washing the utensils and cookware in silence, and I was grateful for his quiet companionship. Our task complete, we hauled the supplies back to camp, where Rollins ordered them to be packed onto the mule. When the final preparations were complete, I watched in fascination as forty soldiers lined up. A band of rabble they were certainly not; their arms were polished and shiny in the dappled morning sunlight. While many militia outfits did not sport matching uniforms, this group of Nelson's best wore sharp blue waistcoats and clean tan breeches. All of the men wore an unvarying, neat queue in their hair—not a wig to be seen. They stood straight, tall, and proud—their attention wholly focused on their commanding officer.

Douglas and his kin were lined up as well—the only men left outside of the formation were Jonas and Rollins.

I stopped at Jonas's side. "What is our plan?"

Jonas looked at me sideways, exasperated. "*Our* plan is to march into town and challenge Campbell and Norrington with superior numbers and firepower—and possibly an empty threat of the justice system."

He glanced at Rollins, who grinned maliciously.

Jonas continued, "*Your* plan is to go home and await our return when this is over."

I glanced around at our small army and shook my head. "I don't think so."

Douglas snickered from his place in the line. Rollins wasn't nearly so discreet. His guffaw was so loud I was sure Norrington himself probably sat up in his bed wondering from whence the sound came.

"Oh, Blake." He slapped Jonas on the shoulder. "Let her come with us! No harm will come to her."

Jonas turned toward me and attempted to burn me down with his blue stare. I measured his stubbornness ounce for ounce. At length he capitulated, drawing a deep breath.

"We will compromise," he said. "You will ride to town with me, and I will deposit you in a safe location *away from the fight.* Is that amenable?"

I nodded.

He gripped my chin and forced me to meet his eyes. "You *will* stay where I leave you, Anne. Is that clear?"

A slow smile spread on my lips.

He squeezed my chin. "Stop that. It won't work. Do you agree, or am I tying you to this tree?"

I hesitated, taking in his features. His lips were pursed together, and his grip on my face was gentle, but his eyes were quite cold. Truly, he wasn't going to budge. "Oh, very well," I sighed, exasperated. "I agree."

Jonas smirked as he lithely tossed me onto his horse and mounted behind me. Securing one hand on the reins and the other on my waist, he nodded at Rollins, who could barely contain his mirth. When Rollins's laughter died out, he gave a shout and the formation fell out in twos, marching out of the clearing and south toward town.

Rollins rode first, closely followed by Douglas, who had requisitioned my horse. Jonas and I followed, leading the men. When Rollins drew ahead of us by several yards, I asked Jonas why we were allowed to ride, rather than proceed on foot.

"His dislike for me isn't based on the facts, Anne. It's mostly air. When the high talk is stripped aside, Rollins and I respect one another."

"Is that so? He called you a *rake*," I informed him with relish.

Jonas chuckled. "Mmm…and you said exactly what to this insult?"

"Only that you are an excellent leader and soldier—and that Douglas following you here is a testament to that fact."

"Thank you for the vote of confidence, Miss Anne."

I sighed. "Do you think this will go well, Jonas?"

He hesitated before answering, but when he did, his voice was steady. "Yes, I do, Anne."

Our ride into Abbingdon was of short duration. The edges of town were barely visible in the early dawn light. Jonas spurred his mount off the road to an abandoned shed fifty yards away. He stopped the horse, awaiting my dismount, but I didn't move.

He sighed. "Anne…"

"But…"

He whipped my face around and kissed me ferociously, stopping any form of protest. I was seated in front of him and could neither pull away nor grip him with my arms. And to be truthful, his kiss was so well timed and skillful, I forgot my stubbornness. After a few breathless moments, he pulled away and set me firmly down on the ground.

"Now, get inside that shed and stay put," he said.

I took my place in the open doorway of the shoddy building and pouted.

Jonas grinned, pleased with himself, and wheeled his horse about. As he rode out toward the road I began to panic, unreasonably worried that he wouldn't make it back.

"Jonas!" I called. "I do love you!"

He halted long enough to glance back at me over his shoulder. The warmth and devotion pouring from his face set me up quite well for the rest of the morning.

The problem was, sitting still while some important events were unfolding in town was not an easy task for me. And besides, there was naught to do in that dusty old shed but sit, and nowhere to sit, at that. It was just a dirty old place that most likely used to house somebody's farm tools. An abandoned chicken coop sat inside—a fairly large, well-built one from the looks of it. A worn sign on scrap wood was affixed above the door—its letters scrawled by an honest and uneducated hand: "This Wass the Hoame of Mrs. Jenkins."

Surely that was a good omen, right? To be relegated to the hallowed home of the most famed bantam in Sussex County must carry strong weight, indeed, with the providential forces at work that day.

I sat down on the step and put my chin in my hands.

Then I stood and walked around the circumference of the shed.

And then I walked two yards from the shed toward the road, admittedly feared Jonas's wrath, and returned to the shed.

And then, finally, I resumed my seat on the step of the shed.

And that was only the first seven minutes—barely long enough for Jonas to even get into town, much less the forty men marching from the grove.

I began to pray, because that was a fine idea, and because I knew God was with us. But my prayers led me to *think* about the fight and to *think* about Campbell and Norrington and Jonas and Douglas, and my mind veered off course into anxiety. For a few minutes, I considered just walking back to the farm, but that was a poor idea on many counts. First of all, I would have to walk through town, in which I would find a mighty heap of trouble. Second, it was near on four miles if not more, and I was beyond the point of exhaustion. I had not slept all night—again. *Would I ever sleep a normal night again?* I wondered. And third, if Jonas returned to find me gone, he would fret about me terribly and then be angry when he found me.

No, for certain this old shed was the best place for me, but I had a pride problem that prevented me from waiting peacefully.

It occurred to me directly that the shed was tucked far back in the woods and that there was a path (spotted during my circumnavigation of the shed) that led through the woods in the general direction of town. This detour would meander in a circuitous route and not directly through the brawl; it was a safe route, to be sure. Once I walked for a while, I could cut through the woods back to the village center as I wished, undetected. After all, Abbingdon was quite small—barely two-dozen buildings grouped together around a village center—just near where I so nearly killed Will Norrington several weeks past.

I rose from my perch and crept to the path, telling myself that I wasn't planning to actually *go and see* the fight—I just wanted to get close enough to hear something, anything. Skirting the edge of town to overhear the altercation was *not exactly* disregarding Jonas's instructions.

Valiantly ignoring the nerves in my stomach, I followed the path through the woods for several minutes. At length it turned due west and left the forest behind it at the back of a building. The distinct brickwork around the top of the building indicated that I was behind the post office. A short alley to my left would deposit me directly at the square.

I was far outside of the realm of obedience now, so far away from the shed that Jonas would not see me if he returned. And yet I heard shouts coming from the town square and had not the strength to turn back from the action.

My ears perked up when I distantly heard the words *Summerton Farm.* I also recognized the name *Nate Wilkins,* which caused no end of pain in my chest and prompted me to edge a few yards closer to the post office. The corner of the building obscured the scene of the action. But from this vantage point I could hear almost everything.

"You, sir, are outside of the realm of the law!" That was Rollins.

"The law? There is no law here, save for me!" Norrington replied.

A cacophony of shouts erupted and muffled the next exchange.

When the clamor subsided, Rollins spoke again, "I have acquaintances in Williamsburg who would be mighty interested in this operation you have going here, Norrington—not to mention the death of an innocent boy."

Although I could not see Norrington, I could only imagine his fleshy face growing red with anger as he sputtered his response.

"I did not murder Nate Wilkins! It was a brawl that got out of hand!" His voice made me shudder with anger and disgust.

"But as no arrests were made, the man who did the killing was suspiciously above the law. Isn't that so?" My own Tom's voice added to the fray.

Well done, Tom!

Norrington faltered. He had nothing to say.

"And you, sir," Rollins continued, "what right have you to be here in the middle of this? Are you a resident of Abbingdon, sir?"

Logan Campbell answered, matching Rollins's bravado inch by inch, "No, sir, I am not. I simply came to Abbingdon to deliver the militia's property safely back into its hands."

Property? Could he mean Jonas? He will not stand to be called such. I leaned ever closer to the corner of the building to see if a view was afforded me.

Indeed, I could hear Jonas shouting in response and several other voices joining in the verbal warfare but could not discern their words. So I took to praying once again. *God, this is the time when we need you the most. I beg you, allow not one of my loved ones to be harmed, or killed…and somehow, if you please, a good crop this year would also be mighty helpful.*

I did not feel the automatic peace that praying often yielded. In reality, I felt that if my burden wasn't significantly lightened, I should crumple under its weight. The erratic pace of the past fortnight had given me little time to react to the pressure. The adventure to fetch

Jonas, coupled with my anguished return home, only to again throw myself into the throngs of this conflict, left me with no opportunity to adapt or to regain strength.

My prayers and reflection were interrupted by three simultaneous sounds: hoof beats, leading away toward the south; musket fire; and voices shouting Jonas's name.

Knowing the danger yet ignoring it, feeling the pressure yet bearing it, I stumbled the last several yards out of the alley into the bright village square. I was assaulted by a myriad of sights, both encouraging and dreadful.

First, Logan Campbell and all of his Scottish rogues were nowhere to be seen.

Second, a few men lay on the ground, unmoving; I could not see their faces to determine their identity.

Third, Norrington's ringleader, Ben Cummings, was being locked into the stocks in the center of the square. He was rendered motionless, held at musket point by two of Rollins's men.

Fourth, Jonas was gone.

Really, the first and third were highly cheering, the second dreadful, while the fourth was insupportable. I glanced about furtively, scanning the perimeter of the square for some sign of Jonas or his horse but saw nothing to give me hope. As this dismal truth settled, another alarming notion rushed to the forefront of my mind.

Norrington was curiously absent from the scene.

There was no time to react as I was jerked sharply from behind, back into the darkness of the alley. A piercing squeal escaped my lips as I wriggled about to face my captor. I was not surprised to learn his identity.

It was Norrington's arms that were clasped about my waist, clutching me tightly. He proceeded to slam me into the wall of the post office. As my head crashed against the brick, sharp pricks of pain cascaded down my back.

"Norrington!" I gasped. "Unhand me at once!"

His face was a fearsome sight to behold; his cheeks—usually puffy to begin with—were blotchy, the skin tight and shiny. His forehead was slick with sweat, and his countenance held such an expression of rage that I lost all traces of the bravado I'd taken to displaying.

"I'll do no such thing," he snarled, gripping my arms. "If not for you, none of this would have happened. What in the devil do you mean, bringing the militia down on my head? Do you know what I ought to do to you, Miss Summerton?"

On the surface I was astonished that he would manhandle me in this way. But beneath my anger simmered a justified fear. My hiding place was too well concealed. If the soldiers didn't notice me before the shots were fired, they would not notice me now. Indeed, we were alone in the shadows of the alley—the attentions of my allies focused elsewhere—and Norrington emitted a wrath that was not to be waylaid.

I screamed for aid, but the sound was quickly trapped beneath Norrington's hand.

His mood began to transform from anger to something more sinister, as he slid his free hand behind my back, his arm forming an iron-like vise around my small frame. He leaned closer to speak in my ear. "You know, Miss Summerton—*Anne.*" He whispered, "In a way, this ploy of mine has always been about Summerton. That piece of land on which you sit is too magnificent to be mishandled by a young woman."

Fury shot through me as I wriggled to escape. He was adding insult to rapidly increasing injury. I tried to feed the fury so that it would burn through my fear and help me to think clearly. However, Norrington's proximity had the opposite effect on me, increasing the panic a hundredfold.

"The land, yes, I've always wanted your land. But you, Anne, with your spirit and fire, have been as much of a prize as your farm."

He loosened his grip on my arms, but still leaned in close, his breath hot on my neck. We were close enough to the end of the alley, but I would need to wrest myself free to attract anybody's attention. It was difficult enough to walk the fine line between calm control and outright panic, and the further movement of Norrington's hand was erasing my thin reserve of calm quickly enough. The hair on my arms stood straight on end, and I began to tremble violently. He placed a fleshy palm to my cheek, grinning as he spoke. "You know, Miss Summerton, I believe—"

The deafening crack of close range musket fire interrupted Norrington's statement. At once a shriek of pain escaped his lips, but not before a sickening crunch indicated that the musket ball had found its mark. Norrington sank to the cobblestones, writhing in agony and holding the gaping hole where his kneecap had been.

I retained my calm long enough to glance toward the mouth of the alley to discern the source of the shot. With abject relief, my gaze rested upon my brother Tom, a musket at his side and a grim smile on his face. His one available shot had turned out to be the most important.

He stretched his hand out to me. "It's okay now, Annie. Come."

My legs would not obey Tom, as my imminent breakdown finally found its release. The strain of the previous day's trauma won its battle with my calm, and I collapsed in a bloodstained heap by Norrington's side.

When I awoke it was dark—not simply end-of-the-day dark, but midnight dark. I was blessedly in my own bed. There was a stillness in my room that defied description. Perhaps it was my long absence that had caused my things and furniture to appear lifeless until my return. Or maybe a gloom had enshrouded my home since Father died, and the air in my room was simply paying its respects. Probably, it was the dark mood that usually plagued me during the waking hours, combined with the detachment from the world I'd experienced when I fainted.

My body was clean, my hair loose and untangled, and my nightgown on and laced to my neck. All of those things were exceedingly comforting to me, though I had no memory of being cleaned, brushed, dressed, or brought to my home. In fact, the last thing I remembered was wondering which of the dead bodies strewn on the ground belonged to Jonas, and I thus began to whimper in the darkness.

It couldn't be called crying; I had no energy for that. No, it was truly a whimper, just the dread I'd accrued in rest leaking from my mouth as I breathed. There wasn't even feeling left to ask God what had happened—true, I'd seen Norrington defeated, but did Jonas pay the price for that victory? If I'd had the opportunity to choose between victory over Norrington and a long and happy life for Jonas (not even with—I wouldn't even demand that), which would I choose?

These were dark thoughts indeed, perfect for the dark stillness in my silent room—silent but for my sad whimpering.

Between clenched sobs I heard a stirring from beside me on the floor. Thinking it was a rat, I sat up, clutched my quilt, and peered over the edge of the bed—fully prepared to see a rodent to make my horror complete.

I was surprised to see not a rat, but Jonas Blake lying on my floor and rubbing his eyes.

"Anne?" he whispered. "Are you finally awake?"

Obviously, I cried out—in fear, relief, or whatever general overload of emotion is readily available at such a moment. I fell back against my pillows, agitated beyond comprehension, sobbing fully. Jonas immediately came to my side, pulling me into his arms in order to re-establish my serenity.

"Anne! Hush, dearest. All is well! There is no reason to cry. All of your hopes are restored. Please ... it is late, and Tom and Betsy are sleeping. Shhh ... shh ... "

I paused my sobbing long enough to gasp. "You were gone. I heard musket fire, and you were … gone!"

"Yes, I was gone after *you*, goose," he said, tugging at my hair. "As soon as the first shot was fired, I was away from there, riding to the shed to find you in case one of Campbell's men rode awry in the woods and came upon you."

My sobs receded in the realization—was it possible? That everything had indeed worked out as I'd hoped?

"Of course, you were nowhere to be seen," Jonas said.

I nodded into his shirt. "I'm sorry." My voice was muffled. "I have no worthwhile excuse."

"No, you don't," Jonas answered, sitting upright and loosening my grasp on his neck. He stared down at me for a few minutes, so obviously as tired as I was. His pale face was marked with circles beneath his eyes. His brow was furrowed, displaying his cross disposition.

"Please, Jonas," I whispered, pulling at his arm, "don't go."

At length a small smile broke his stern mask. He pushed me back onto the pillows, arranging the quilt at my shoulders and gently stroking my hair. Then he reached down to the floor and fetched the blanket he'd been using. "See here, Anne," he said, "I love you dearly, but I am a man of honor, such as I can be. Unless I am your husband, I am not authorized by God to share your bed. So I will gladly lie here next to you but will stay above the coverlet, if you please."

I smiled in the dark, marveling at his ready answers and thorough sense of honor. In so many ways he had changed in two years; in this way, he had not. He lay down facing me, atop my blankets but under the old quilt Mother always had folded at the foot of my bed. I nestled my head against his chest and wrapped one arm around his back, sighing contentedly.

"So?" I whispered, trying to delay my exhaustion to hear what was likely a wonderfully entertaining story.

"So, what?" Jonas asked.

" What happened in the square?"

"Oh, that," he remarked, tracing his fingers up and down my spine. "Well, Norrington and Campbell blustered a good deal, plainly accustomed to scaring people into getting their own way, but they'd never met the likes of Major Rollins." He chuckled. "They didn't know what to do with Rollins and his threats, much less his troops. It was really no contest, Anne."

He paused to brush his lips against my forehead, while I marveled at how my outlook had changed so dramatically within the space of five minutes.

"Once Rollins threw around the threat of calling the governor down here, preoccupied as he is with the war, Campbell turned tail out of there. I suspect he has already garnered some attention by the governor down in North Carolina. Anyhow, while he and his men rode out, one of Norrington's men started shooting, welcoming the distraction, you know."

My entire body tensed with the thought of open gunfire in that place, but Jonas smoothed my hair and patted my back to calm me down once again.

"There was no danger," he whispered. "That man Ben Cummings is a terrible shot. I was out of range by then anyway, off to the north of town to find you."

He paused, and I surmised that his face was dark and severe once more.

"Um, go on," I said.

"Well, ah, after not finding you at the shed ... *where I asked you to stay ...* "

"Let it rest, Jonas."

But when he continued, his voice was jovial and teasing. " ... I rode back into town, only to find Ben in the stocks and the rest of his men chained to the post office. Tom informed me of what transpired in the alleyway and with great and deserved pride showed me the hole in Norrington's leg. You were in a heap at the end of the alley." At this point in the story, his voice turned worried, his arm tightening around my waist. "You were breathing, but I couldn't rouse you, so I brought you back here quickly and gave you to Betsy. She shooed me out of the room."

I grinned at the picture.

"When she left your room a while later, she said you were sleeping and forced me to take a bath and have something to eat." I felt his shoulders shrug. "And then I came up here and laid down on the floor, waiting for you."

"I thought you were dead." I sniffled. "And Norrington…" A shudder rippled through me. "I imagine it was finally just too much strain. I have no recollection of Betsy bathing or dressing me."

Jonas's voice was hard. "I can't even turn my thoughts toward that scoundrel without wishing all sorts of ill on him. Let me just say that if I had found you, and not Tom, Will Norrington would be having his reckoning with God, rather than nursing a leg wound in the gaol."

I could find no ready dissent to his harsh statement. Instead, I yawned, and Jonas joined me.

"We are both quite tired," he remarked. "Do you not think so?"

"Is that a signal to quiet my questions so we can sleep?"

"It could be."

"Will you be here when I awake?"

"Dearest Anne." Jonas tightened his hold on me. "I aim not to leave you again."

I wanted to ask him what he meant, because technically he was still in the militia, but the warmth of the bed, the comfort of his presence, and the release of the tension and fears of many months finally won.

It was fitting that Jonas and I, not having really slept for days, would finally find rest together. A few times throughout the night I awoke in a panic, only to feel his arm around me tighten and his breathing steady. I would fall again into the best sleep I believe I'd had in years.

IN WHICH JONAS AND I
REACH ANOTHER ACCORD

Jonas wasn't completely honest. First of all, when I awoke the next morning, he was not there.

And second, he did indeed leave me again, for the war needed good men, and it could not tarry.

Although he was not in my room at sunup, I heard loud voices and laughter from the parlor and fancied he was close. I decided, after sleeping most of the previous day and the entire night, that I might bear getting up and dressing. Laying hands on a dress and a brush, I quickly cleaned myself and then sat on my bed, pausing for reflection.

I stayed in that position for quite a long time. My body's immobility was a result of a combination of factors: fatigue, surely, but beyond that it was a sense of tranquility after so many weeks of striving, not only with my body, but with my mind. Somehow, amazingly, my mind could be at rest. It was difficult to grasp, awaking today and not needing to worry or fret for the future.

Laughter filtered up the stairs, breaking through my thoughts. I rose from the bed, patted my hair, and, wearing my last good dress, trotted down the stairs.

In the parlor I saw the reason for all of my toil—my small family, Tom and Betsy, and my new, expanded family, the McLeans. Realizing those men had fought for me and mine, filled my heart with such warmth I could barely contain it—I nearly had to return to my room and weep.

The McLeans were gathered around our parlor, their huge frames occupying more space than we possessed. Betsy was happily serving them steaming mugs of tea and fresh-baked bread, and it seemed to me that James received rather a larger serving than the rest. I smiled at the thought of Betsy with James and Tom with Mary.

And what of Jonas and me?

Jonas stood across the room from me at the kitchen door. I met his glance; he nodded toward the door and ambled through it. I followed him, skirting the edge of the parlor to avoid detection.

He meandered toward the north pasture to our favorite tree where we'd spent many a day talking, laughing, and poring over his old Bible. I wordlessly slid my hand into his, and in peace and silence we walked across the farm. *My* farm.

When we reached the tree, Jonas plopped to the ground. He attempted to pull me down next to him, but I stubbornly stood my ground.

"Oh, no," I said, hands on my hips, "I have ruined not one, not two, not even three, but *four* dresses at your hand, Jonas Blake, and do you know that this is indeed my last one? I cannot fathom what I'll wear tomorrow!"

Jonas's eyes grew wide with amusement. He swiftly leaned forward, grasped me about the waist, and pulled me onto his lap. "There," he said. "Your frock is still clean, my dear."

I struggled very little against him, hard-pressed to find fault in sitting on Jonas's lap. Indeed, I quite enjoyed the pleasant placement. "But what of my others?" I complained.

Jonas pressed his forehead to mine. "I will buy you four dresses, and more besides, after I return from the war with a fancy title and commission."

After he returned from the war. I could think of nothing to say in response.

He cleared his throat. "Major Rollins has given me a few days to stay with you and regain my strength. After that I will be leaving again, Anne."

This news was no surprise to me, and yet it saddened me all the same. I was unable to enjoy the moment with him; instead, my eyes traveled across the many acres of Summerton Farm that would remain fallow until the war was over. Even without the added strain of Norrington's tyranny, we still had nobody to help us with the mounds and mounds of labor required to run the place.

Jonas misread my sadness. "I'll be back, Anne. And when I return, if you'll have me, we will be married."

My distress momentarily stayed, I pulled away from him—a heady mixture of surprise and bliss. "Jonas, did you say *married?*"

He laughed, taking advantage of the moment to kiss me sweetly on the forehead. "Yes, Anne, I did. Does that surprise you? Did I not make my feelings and intentions very clear?"

I considered this question seriously. He had actually caused me a fair bit of confusion on the matter, with his brusque, dismissive ways. Sometimes a day would elapse without him speaking to me, and then he would suddenly exhibit an unnatural level of protectiveness. My silence told Jonas that the answer wasn't so plain.

"Well, Anne, don't keep me in suspense!"

"Jonas, at first you were a bit standoffish, you know. And then you were, well, a fair bit concerned for me, but not overly talkative."

His blue eyes narrowed; his lips pursed in frustration. Jonas tightened his arm around my waist, gripping my chin with his free hand. "Anne!" his voice was plainly exasperated now. "Need I count how many days our lives have been in danger during this past fortnight? Should I reacquaint you with those memories? Life and death circumstances leave very little room for paying romantic attentions, wouldn't you say?"

"Yes"—I nodded against his palm— "but..."

"Yes?"

"You were angry when I first arrived."

Jonas sighed, relaxing his aggravated hold on my body. "Yes, I was. Wait … no, I wasn't. Not angry. Just vexed that my assumptions were false."

"Assumptions about what?"

"I was certain I'd successfully forgotten all about you, but"—he paused, brushing his lips against my cheek softly— "when I saw you that night in the camp, I knew I was mistaken, and it was a sound beating to my pride to know that two years hadn't changed how I felt about you."

I smiled a little. "So you still loved me?"

He returned my smile. "Yes, you goose. Of course."

My emotions began to overflow once again, and I gripped his collar, sobbing gratefully for the blessings that had occurred that day.

Jonas cocked his head and stared at me. "What are you blubbering for?"

I paused. "I don't rightly know."

He chuckled. "I am attempting, again, to ask you to wait for me, but you won't stop crying."

I stared at him, wiping the ever-present tears from my face.

"So, Anne? Will you wait for me?"

I answered him with a much-anticipated, long-overdue kiss on his sassy, sardonic mouth, and it was magnificent.

Jonas's "few days of leave" stretched into a week, and I'm not ashamed to say I put him to work to make him earn his keep. Indeed, he moved back into his regular place in the barn for the time, and he was not alone. James decided to stay on for the summer, for more reasons than one, although the extra pair of hands on the farm was so useful I cared not what his motives were.

Major Rollins, as unsavory as his reputation may have been, made good on all of his promises and more besides. He disposed of all traces of outstanding warrants or bad service reports for not only Jonas, but for all of the McLeans as well, which just goes to show

how a common enemy can unite polar opposites in a surprising way. He also kept his promise to march Norrington and his cronies to Williamsburg, which he did with great fanfare, and deposited those men into the judgment that God faithfully promised me from the Scriptures.

At the end of that short and joyful week, Jonas and I sat on the porch of the house, mentally cursing the heat but enjoying respite from a long hard day. The silence of the impending twilight was deafening and comforting after such a day of hard labor, and we drank it in companionably while the dusk was ushered in.

Jonas turned to me, the fleeing sunlight creating flickering shadows on his face. "Anne?"

"Hmm?" My eyes roamed the fields.

"Are you glad I came back?"

I faced him, hoping he could see the emotion and joy behind the smile that crossed my face. "Of course I am, Jonas. I can't thank you enough for how you have changed my life. God brought you back to me, and you brought me back to God."

The thoughtful silence fell on us again for a few minutes.

"And anyway," I continued, "I came to fetch *you*, remember?"

He scoffed. "I would have returned eventually."

"And drawn my father's ire?"

His blue eyes were amused. "Your father had no ire—that was your mother. He would have come around."

Remembering my father's words at his death, I nodded, keeping the secret safe in my heart—for the time being.

"I imagine so."

Moments later our peace was interrupted by footsteps approaching the lane to the house. We looked up in surprise.

"Captain Blake?" Two soldiers hailed us from the gate.

From what I saw of the regulars in the Virginia militia, these men were more important than the average minuteman—in any case, they were better dressed. They walked up the long path to where Jonas and I sat.

"Yes?" Jonas asked, confidence suddenly blazing from him.

"We have instructions to take you north to the Continental Army to receive new orders, Captain."

The Continental Army? That explained the stately nature of these men—they likely came straight from Washington himself! I fancied they did, anyway. So Rollins had made a gentleman officer out of Jonas after all. We would be indebted to him for that.

"New orders?" Jonas and I said. Of course, I said them with worry and fear; Jonas said them with excitement and anticipation.

"Yes, sir. Lafayette has arrived, you know, and we are laying plans for further offensives against the British."

Jonas and I looked at each other for a long moment. His eyes flickered around the farm—where he would someday, hopefully, return—and back to my face. They flashed to the proud, majestic men that stood next to us. His face broke into a wide and satisfied grin.

"Well, let's go north, then! I'm terribly bored with farm work!" This last was uttered with a sprightly wink at me over his shoulder.

A great sigh escaped me, but I covered it with bravery and fixed a lofty smile on my face. The messengers cleared their throats and turned their backs to us discreetly. Jonas faced me and encircled me with his arms.

"Godspeed, Jonas," I said. "Fight well so you can return to me."

"No fears, Anne Summerton, do you hear me? God holds us in the palm of his hand."

I nodded. "I will remember."

He kissed me, and it was the type of kiss that foretold a long absence and many nights of loneliness. I squeezed back my anxious tears as he pulled away.

"I love you," he said.

I grinned and tightened my arms around him once again. He squeezed me gently and then released me, turning to the soldiers.

As they started down the lane, I watched the three of them walking jauntily toward battle and pondered the courage of men. It was important for Jonas to be needed and valuable—something in him demanded it—and his valor came from the satisfaction of that need being met.

I also pondered the courage of women, for we possessed it as well—only it often had to be buried, or at least deferred, in order to allow our men to be the brave ones. The laws of our colony did not afford women an opportunity to be courageous, but in the lawless days of the war, women were slowly beginning to assume men's roles. I had heard of a woman who masqueraded as a man and fought in the Massachusetts militia and of countless others that served as spies for both sides. Those women made me beam with pride. They had found their chance to be brave, and had seized it. And in a smaller way, I had done so as well.

Jonas Blake walked away from me, proud, resplendent with joy and excitement. He turned at the gate, gazing at me affectionately once more, and waved good-bye.